The Hummingbird and the Hawk

The Hummingbird and the Hawk

Charles B. Pettis

BOOKLOGIX®

Alpharetta, GA

10 9 8 7 6 5 4 3 2   0 1 2 6 1 5

ISBN: 978-1-61005-416-4

Illustrations by Michelle Phillips / www.michelecreates.com

Printed in the United States of America

∞This paper meets the requirements of ANSI/NISO Z39.48-1992 (Permanence of Paper)

If we wonder often,
the gift of knowledge will come.

—*Native American Proverb*

Contents

The Story of the Stories

You hold in your hands a book of stories about a magical place and time that surely existed here on earth. Perhaps it does still.

And how did these stories come about? What is their genesis? I'll explain.

We were visiting with friends over a Labor Day weekend—one of those long weekends that includes a Thursday and a Monday. For some reason, our conversation turned to things ecological and things avian. Sue had a suggestion for me. Sue—she's the one who went on early morning "birding" walks while we were students at Miami University—mentioned that over the past several decades the populations of hawks and hummingbirds have been decreasing steadily in the continental United States. Because I write a little from time to time, Sue thought I should do some research and produce a paper on the subject. I demurred. That is to say, I made it clear that I don't work that way. Most all my stuff is pure imagination. With that, I figured the subject was at an end.

Upon returning home, the words hawk and hummingbird started echoing somewhere in my brain. And that echo led me to my PC where, over a

few days' time, I produced the story from which the title of this book is taken.

My wife Berta and our good friend Steve Checkosky read the story and pronounced it a hit. I thought it was pretty good too, so I was batting 1.000. Why would I want to broaden the poll and risk diminishing my average! And I was satisfied with the one story. You need to understand, though, that Berta is very good at encouraging me to write. Sometimes she gets just a jot pushy, and her encouragement morphs into something more. But her heart is always in the right place.

In time, the muse took over once again, and I produced the story of Shinaka, the great hawk. The same self-appointed editorial board read and approved of the story, and more "encouragement" came my way. Well, you get the idea.

I learned something from this project. The muse sure helps to tweak my brain and helps me choose words. But there is nothing quite as energizing as a good, swift kick in the seat of the pants!

Thanks then to Sue and Tom Wagner and to Linda and Bob Weisflog, whose friendship got me started. Another nod to Stephen F. Checkosky, PhD. Our friend Steve, who, without saying it, let me know it was my *responsibility* to continue writing this series of stories. And of course, thanks to Berta, my wife and best friend, for all her encouragement.

Acknowledgments

I n addition to the six people mentioned under "The Story of the Stories," there are a few others who deserve a hearty "Thank You!"

To my project manager, Jessica, who kept things rolling, even while I was working on those last revisions. To Kelly, my editor, who refused to let just *any words* appear in the book. To Michele, whose artwork brings a fresh, enduring touch to the book. To Ellina and Laura, who designed a book that is even a joy to hold and to look at. To Ahmad, who directs this intrepid crew, and who always has a smile on his face and time for a few kind words.

A special thank-you to my good friend Jack, who reads all my stuff—even when it's not so good. His subtle suggestions gave me a new perspective on these stories.

And to you, adventurous reader, who decided to pick up this book and read at least this far, I say, "Thank you." And add, "What are you waiting for? Turn the page and get started!"

THE HUMMINGBIRD AND THE HAWK

THE HUMMINGBIRD AND THE HAWK

"Tell me the story again, my grandfather. Please tell it once again."

"But it was only yesterday I told it to you. And it has been twice you have asked to hear it since the great yellow moon last made her way across the sky."

"If you tell the story now, I won't ask for a very long time. I promise." Smiling Fawn flashed her best smile at the old man.

Brave Wolf was intent on making a long leather strap, but he was never too busy for his favorite grandchild. She was the daughter of his son, Strong Wolf, and only in the seventh year of her life. Strong Wolf and his wife, White Sparrow, had brought Smiling Fawn into the world when they were both in their fortieth year, an unexpected event to be sure. And it was the joyous laughter of the little child that led to her name.

"So," said Brave Wolf as he laid his work to one side and brushed small pieces of leather from his deerskin shirt, "you want to hear about the hummingbird once again?"

"Yes. Oh, and the hawk, too. They go together, don't they, Grandfather?"

"Well, in the story they do. You must remember that."
He thought about saying more, but her expectant face and
his good sense ended his speech there.

Brave Wolf rose from his mat, took Smiling Fawn by the
hand, and led her to a log bench outside his lodge. It was
early autumn, and the sun shone proudly in a cloudless
sky. From the bench, they could look down the long path
that wound among the many lodges in the village. The last
of the wild flowers bloomed in front of each lodge: red,
yellow, purple, violet, blue, pink, and some almost black.
From the blossoms, the Armaha made dyes that decorated
their clothing and colored their woven mats.

When they were settled on the bench, Brave Wolf said,
teasing his granddaughter, "Let us see, how does the story
begin . . . ?"

"Many years ago, in the time before . . ." Smiling
Fawn began for him, all the while tugging at his sleeve.

"Oh, yes, that is how it starts," he said. He pulled her
a little closer to him and began.

Many years ago, in the time before our people
came to this land, and before other tribes came to
this land, there lived in a beautiful valley a great
hawk. Among the animals, she was known by the
name Shinaka, and she was a magnificent creature.
She was almost as tall as you and had the most
beautiful feathers of gray, brown, black, and white
that shimmered in the sun. Shinaka's head was
covered with feathers of bright orange, and her eyes
were yellow, no, golden. Yes, her eyes were golden.

Shinaka was queen of the skies in the valley, keeping watch so that the other animals and birds were safe. When she hunted for food, she flew to places far distant from her valley because all the creatures in her valley lived in peace and harmony. If one of the animals or birds in her valley could not find food, Shinaka would search and then tell them where to look. Oh, yes, life was peaceful and good in the valley.

The rains came to the valley and brought life-giving water for all. And for three months each year, the snow fell in the far mountains to feed the streams and rivers that coursed down their steep, rocky sides and flowed into this valley and all the other valleys. In the summer, Brother Sun kept the air warm, and when he had flown to his nightly rest, giving way to Sister Moon, gentle breezes stirred the air easily—enough so the animals and birds could sleep without care.

Spring and autumn days were a little cool—though never cold—and all the creatures sought protected places to sleep, places away from the wind that often rose in the night. In winter, many of the birds flew away from the valley in search of warmer days and nights. It is told that some birds fly greater distances than the buffalo herds travel. The larger animals, as they do today, found refuge in caves in the lower slopes of the mountains to sleep until awakened by the warmth of spring.

And over all this, Shinaka kept her watch, silently noting the whereabouts of all her creatures, for that was her place in life, her role as prescribed by the Great One.

5

Smiling Fawn could contain herself no longer. "And where is the Great One, Grandfather? You speak of him but you never tell me where he is."

"And have I ever said the Great One is a man?"

The little girl realized the truth of what he had said and shook her head. "No, but I just thought that it was a 'he' and not a 'she.'"

"Because we say 'great,' you think it is a man," said Brave Wolf. "But we have Sister Moon to guide us when Brother Sun sleeps. And we have Mother Earth to thank for the bounty of our fields. You see, the Great One could be either man or woman. But we are getting away from our story. Let me see . . ."

Smiling Fawn wrapped her arms around his right arm and smiled at the wrinkled face she loved so very much.

One fine spring day, Shinaka was soaring high near the face of the mountain we now call Umaqua, the Sacred House. As she rose and turned away from the mountain, she spied a small speck in the sky. Whatever it was, it was flying, but Shinaka had never seen such a small creature flying so fast, and never near her valley. She soared high in the sunlit sky to look at this tiny wonder from above.

And what a sight it was. This little being, this tiny being, flapping its wings so hard and fast they were a blur. Shinaka was blessed with keen sight and hearing, and what she heard was new, amazing, almost from another world. She heard a buzzing sound coming from whatever was flying over her

valley. Her eyes told her it was a bird—a bird that buzzes like Sister Bee!

The buzzing thing saw Shinaka's shadow, stopped right where it was in the middle of the air, and darted into the top of a lodgepole pine tree. The hawk had never seen any creature do such a thing. The hawk flew silently to another pine tree nearby and watched. In due time, the little flying thing took to the air and flew right in front of Shinaka, not a wing's length away. The hawk was so startled she almost lost the grip she had on the branch. She did get a closer look, and it—whatever it was—had a long sharp nose, and was green with a small dot of red somewhere on its tiny body.

Shinaka watched as the little flying thing sought out a bush with bright orange flowers. It stuck its nose deep into the flowers, beating its wings to hold itself in place. After a very short time, the little creature darted to another flower, then another, until it had poked its nose into almost all the flowers on that bush. Then it flew to the next bush and repeated the darting and nose-sticking. The hawk continued watching for some time. Then she flew down to a low branch near the bushes and decided to find out what sort of "thing" had come to her valley.

"Excuse me," said Shinaka respectfully. You see, she was a hawk who guarded the valley, but she was always polite, especially to elders and to strangers. She had decided it was some sort of bird because it had wings and flew like a bird. There was no answer. Perhaps the little creature had not heard. So she tried

again, this time a little louder. "Excuse me, little green bird, may I speak to you?"

"Oh," was all the tiny green bird could manage. It alit near a flower and settled its tiny wings along its body. "You . . . you took me by surprise . . . I was feeding on these nice flowers . . . I didn't hear you." The little bird was shaking, afraid. Surely the size of the hawk was intimidating, for Shinaka was many times bigger than he.

"There is no need to be nervous or afraid in my presence, little friend. I am Shinaka, the hawk who watches over this valley. You are new to our home, and I have a few questions."

"A few questions?" The little bird imagined he might be a meal if he weren't careful.

"Yes, but only a few. Let's start with an easy one. I have told you who I am, so what is your name, if you have one? And tell me, what *are* you?"

"I am called Nuluk. I am the bird that hums . . . I mean a hummingbird. And you?"

"I am a hawk. May I go on with my questions?" she asked.

"Yes," said Nuluk. "I will try to answer them if I can."

"Will you be in our valley a long time, or are you only passing through—on a journey to some other place?" asked the hawk.

"Well," said Nuluk, rubbing his beak back and forth over a nearby branch, "I am looking for a new home,

and so far, I have found all that I need right here. Tell me, are there more of these flowers in the valley?"

"Yes, all over *our* valley." A bit of emphasis to give the little male bird another idea of who was more important. "You will be staying a long time, then."

"Only until the cold wind comes down and turns the tops of the mountains white," said Nuluk. "Then I'll fly back to where I came from, where it is warm all year."

Shinaka considered this then asked, "Why do you stick your nose into the flowers? Are you smelling them?"

"No, no, Shinaka . . . Is it permissible to call you Shinaka?" She nodded to him and he went on. "You see I am looking for nectar in the flowers. I push my beak all the way to the bottom of each blossom and find the sweet nectar there. That is what I eat mostly—oh, that and a few small bugs from time to time. So I am not smelling the flowers, I am drinking their nectar. And I must say these orange flowers are very tasty, very tasty indeed."

And with that he did a very disrespectful thing. Little Nuluk turned his back on Shinaka, the great hawk, and sipped nectar from two or three other blossoms. The hawk frowned and flapped her wings, rising up on her feet, trying to show the little hummingbird how much bigger she was.

Nuluk sat on a branch and watched the larger bird. He wondered, *Was it wrong to turn my back on the hawk?* Then he said, "Yes, yes, go on. You have other questions?"

"Not for now. Perhaps another time. Tomorrow, maybe." And with that Shinaka rose quickly in the air and made straight for one of her favorite hunting grounds in a canyon a few miles beyond Umaqua.

"But you have added some things this time," said Smiling Fawn as she broke away from Brave Wolf. "I do not remember so many questions the last time you told the story. You should tell it the same every time."

Her grandfather replied with a twinkle in his eye and laughter in his voice, "What good is a story retold if it is without some changes to make it better, more complete?"

"But I want to get to my favorite part of the story . . . the ending."

"And you are afraid that the Great One will be distressed if Smiling Fawn must wait a little longer to hear the ending of a story she has heard many times before?"

"No, he . . . I mean she . . . I mean the Great One will not be distressed, Grandfather. I just . . ."

"The end and the middle of the story will be told in time, little one," said Brave Wolf. "Now come close to me, for the air shows some chill, and I wouldn't want to find you with a runny nose and a cough." With that, Smiling Fawn grabbed his right arm once again and waited for her grandfather to continue the story.

Seven days would pass before Shinaka and Nuluk would meet once again. During that time, Nuluk had flown the length and width of the valley, and just as the

hawk had told him, the bushes with the sweet, orange flowers were in great abundance.

This valley was green and lush with trees to sit on and grasses where small bugs could be found. To Nuluk, it was paradise, and so much different than another valley he had visited only one moon ago. He described it to Shinaka on their second meeting.

"The skies were hazy with dust that the wind lifted from the land," said Nuluk. "The water in the rivers and streams had a peculiar taste."

"Water with a peculiar taste?" asked the hawk. "What do you mean, little friend?"

"The creatures drank the water, but it had something in it that left a strange taste long after it had been sipped, like one had licked a stone or the bark of a tree." He saw the question in Shinaka's eyes. "I know what you are thinking. None of the creatures who lived there had died from drinking that water. They had all come to accept it as quite normal."

"And what sort of animals did you find in this other valley?" asked Shinaka.

"They were much like the animals in this valley, but smaller and much darker in color," he replied. "You see, the water with the funny taste fed the trees, bushes, and grasses. And like the animals, the grass was more gray than green. Even the orange flowers— for they grew there also—were more the color of goat's milk."

"And the nectar?" asked Shinaka.

11

"It was good, but not nearly as sweet as the orange flowers in this valley," said Nuluk. "All the time I was in that other valley I thought it very peculiar, puzzling."

"And how is that?" Shinaka asked.

"None of the creatures seemed the least bit concerned that the water tasted funny, that the sky was always hazy, or that it all seemed so drab. To me it wasn't living—it was merely existing."

"Oh yes!" exclaimed Smiling Fawn. "Now we are coming to the good part, the part about how it all ends!"

"Yes, Smiling Fawn, the end of the story, 'the good part' is almost upon us," said Brave Wolf. "Before I tell it, would you bring me a gourd filled with cool water? With all the telling, my voice is tired. And it needs to be strong to finish the story properly."

The little girl scrambled to her feet and ran to the spring at the edge of the village, smiling all the way. Her grandfather watched her. Such a happy child, he thought. He hoped it would always be so. If not guided with care, a child who greets the world with joy can become quite another person after experiencing more of life.

Smiling Fawn held the green and yellow gourd under the water that flowed gently from the spring, making sure it filled all the way to the top. As she turned to carry the water to the old man, she took two running steps, tripped on a small stone, and went sprawling on the hard ground. The gourd sailed out of her tiny hands, spilling the water, some on the ground and some on her deerskin shirt and leggings. Without a sound,

she got to her feet, brushed the dirt and water from her clothes, picked up the gourd, and went back to the spring. When she had cleaned the gourd and refilled it, Smiling Fawn walked proudly—and a little slower—to her grandfather, smiling all the way.

"Are you all right, little one?" His tone was measured. Too many times the way a question is asked tells what kind of answer is expected. He wanted the young girl to decide how to answer.

"Yes, Grandfather," she said with an extra glow on her face, "I am all right. The water is cool, and the gourd is clean." She held out the gourd, decorated with red and blue markings, and giggled as only Smiling Fawn could.

After taking a few sips of the cool water, Brave Wolf set the gourd aside and said, "Good. Now sit close once more, and I will finish the tale. And I will be careful to tell it just as I did the last time."

She threw her arms around his neck and hugged her beloved grandfather. Smiling Fawn knew she shouldn't make such a public display of affection, but surely the Great One would forgive her. She took her place on her grandfather's right side, held tight to his arm, and waited expectantly.

The story of the other valley disturbed Shinaka greatly. *"How could such a thing happen?"* she wondered. She wanted to understand, and so she asked a question.

"Was there a hawk like me, or perhaps an eagle, to keep watch over that valley?"

"Yes, an eagle," said Nuluk. "He spent all his time making sure he had enough to eat and a suitable place to rest when Sister Moon lighted the sky. I was new to that valley and thought it peculiar, but said nothing to him about it or to any of the other creatures."

"And where is this valley?"

"It is far, far away, where Brother Sun makes his journey low in the sky when the cold winds come," said Nuluk. Then he quickly added, "Surely you are not thinking of going there?"

"No," answered Shinaka. "Tell me, are there many creatures in the valley you tell about?"

"Not as many as in this valley," said Nuluk. "And the creatures I spoke to—the few who were willing to speak—told me there are fewer and fewer creatures as time goes on. Many do not survive when there is snow on the mountains. Others seem to give up."

After a moment to take in what she had just heard, Shinaka asked, "Did you travel to that valley alone, Nuluk?'

"Ah, finally the question most important to you," he said. "You want to know if others like me will come to your valley. I travel with a small flock of hummingbirds. I was sent to find a new home for us. We knew we could not survive in that other, horrible place."

"And when will the other hummingbirds come to our valley?" asked Shinaka.

14

"As soon as I return to them and tell them what I have found," said Nuluk.

"And . . ." prompted Shinaka.

"And I intend to begin my flight tomorrow," said Nuluk, "when Brother Sun is high in the sky. If all goes well, the flock should be feasting on the bright orange flowers of this valley before we see all of Sister Moon once more."

And so it happened as Nuluk said. The small flock of hummingbirds came to the valley. There they prospered until their numbers were too many to count. And they lived out their lives in peace with Shinaka and the other creatures of the valley.

"I like that part, Grandfather," said Smiling Fawn. "It is good to know that the hummingbirds came to the good valley where Shinaka keeps watch."

"Yes, little one," said her grandfather. "It is important to keep watch over Mother Earth so she needn't work so hard. And it is important to watch over one another to make sure all are safe. So it was in Shinaka's valley. Why are you frowning, my granddaughter? Is something bothering you?"

"Where is that valley?" asked the little girl. "I think I would like to visit it one day, maybe even live there."

"But you are already there, my child. Look," said Brave Wolf.

And with that, a great flock of emerald green hummingbirds rose from a row of bushes covered with bright orange flowers. Every so often, a flash of red could be

seen in the flock as it rose in the air and darted this way and that. Then as quickly as it had risen, the flock returned to the same bushes and continued its search for nectar.

Smiling Fawn stared at a nearby pine tree. There in the highest branch she could see a large hawk of gray, brown, black, and white. And its head was covered with orange feathers that shimmered in the bright autumn light.

SHINAKA

SHINAKA

A cold wind swept through the valley and carried new snow to the village. It was winter, and the world was covered in a soft, white blanket. The light from Brother Sun was weak and low in the sky, providing little warmth for the people of the Armaha tribe who lived there. The mountain Umaqua, the Sacred House, was shrouded in clouds that hung far down from the rugged peak.

The Armaha were in their lodges, warmed by the fireplaces in the center of each lodge. The walls of each lodge were made of logs and mud. The flat roof was covered with two or three layers of pine branches laid over saplings. Pine branches and straw were strewn on the dirt floor. Over this, woven mats and skins provided comfort and warmth. A single doorway was cut into one of the long sides of the lodge and covered with a bearskin. Smoke from the central fireplace was drawn out through the single hole in the roof.

The several lodges of the village lined both sides of a wide path that wound among tall oak, pine, and beech trees. At one end of the path, a spring of sweet water from deep inside Mother Earth flowed into a small natural basin among rocks and provided drinking water for the Armaha. The other end of the path, near the forest, separated into three trails. One

trail led to the mountain, Umaqua, and the second to the broad river where fish were caught and clothes were washed. The third trail disappeared into the forest and continued to lands where only hunters dared to travel.

This time of year, the Armaha were busy with tasks that were suitable for the cold days and weeks while Mother Earth rested.

White Sparrow sat near the fire, humming a favorite song while mending a torn sleeping mat. She looked up and smiled lovingly at her husband, something she would never do when among other members of the tribe.

White Sparrow sighed, remembering when she was a young girl and the day she first saw Strong Wolf. He was walking in front of her parents' lodge carrying a wooden pail filled with water from the village spring. She had smiled at him shyly, and without a word, he offered her a sip of the sweet, cold water. She remembered how they both held their breath as she drank, neither one knowing what to say or do. Even now, in the middle years of her life, the memory is clear and enduring; she will hold on to it forever. White Sparrow set the sleeping mat aside and looked around the lodge—their lodge. Yes, all things they possessed were shared, neither his nor hers. And they shared equally and eagerly in raising Smiling Fawn. White Sparrow brushed a strand of graying black hair away from her eyes and once more smiled at her husband.

Strong Wolf had been watching her, so he nodded and smiled in return. As he turned to inspect a worn edge of the bearskin that covered the door, Strong Wolf noticed his young daughter push her sleeping mat from her lap.

Smiling Fawn spoke harshly to the mat. "You are too much trouble. I don't like you!"

Strong Wolf said, "The sleeping mat cannot hear you, my daughter. No matter how much you say to it, the mat will not answer."

"I know," the girl said. "But I have tried and tried to mend it and I cannot . . . it will not . . . it is too hard for me." And she looked as if she might cry.

"Smiling Fawn," said her mother in even tones, "perhaps your grandfather needs a visitor. It has been almost two days since you have been to his lodge."

"It is cold outside, my mother," complained the girl. "The wind blows and makes it even colder. Even Brother Sun looks cold."

"Yes, he does," said Strong Wolf. "He surely looks cold." Strong Wolf smiled and laughed at what his daughter had said. "But your mother is right. It would be good to see your grandfather. And take your mat with you. He may be able to help."

Smiling Fawn frowned, tilted her head to one side, and thought for a moment. At length, she found her warmest cloak and wrapped herself in it. With her sleeping mat held tightly in her hands, she walked to the door of her lodge.

"Be safe, my daughter," said Strong Wolf as he held the bearskin aside, allowing a small breath of winter air to enter the lodge.

Smiling Fawn slipped through the opening, lowered her head, and walked to her grandfather's lodge. It was only a short distance, but the wind and cold made it seem longer.

The girl stood in front of Brave Wolf's lodge and said, "Grandfather, I have come to see you. May I come in?" There was no answer, so she spoke again, this time in a louder voice. "Grandfather, it is Smiling Fawn. May I come in?"

"Oh," came the reply, "yes, little one, yes, come in. But be quick . . . the cold and wind."

Smiling Fawn understood. Quickly, she pushed the bearskin aside, entered the lodge, and made sure the skin was closed properly.

Brave Wolf was sitting on a woven mat, which faced the door of the lodge. It was his favorite, with the head of a large bear woven into it. He held out a hand to his granddaughter. "Come, little one, sit here by my side, close to the fire."

She saw her favorite mat, the one that bore the likeness of the great hawk. As she walked toward her grandfather, Smiling Fawn watched as he smoothed the mat. His hand moved carefully, firmly, making sure the mat was free of ashes or pieces of straw, making sure the image of the hawk could be seen clearly in all its detail. She remembered a few years earlier when her grandfather had let her sit on that mat for the first time. He had told her the hawk would protect her and give her strength. From that day on, when she was in her grandfather's lodge Smiling Fawn always sat on "her" mat. "What have you brought me?" he asked.

"My sleeping mat, Grandfather. It is torn. I want to mend it, but the mat will not do what I want it to do."

"Sleeping mats that do not behave can be much trouble," said Brave Wolf. "Did you push it away and scold it?" She nodded silently. Her grandfather sensed her unhappiness. It

was clear that this little girl needed to think of happier things. "Now, let us not speak of such things as bothersome sleeping mats. Perhaps a story . . ."

"Yes! Yes!" the girl said with excitement in her voice. "And what story will you tell me?"

Brave Wolf said, "You know, I think it will be a story about the great hawk, Shinaka, the one who guards our valley. It is a long story, my granddaughter." He waited.

"I would very much like to hear a story about Shinaka," said Smiling Fawn. She put her torn sleeping mat down and listened.

Gray and green, gray and green, that is all she could see. It was as if she had been transported to some imaginary land, some place that was out of time, out of this world. The feeling was not unfamiliar. In fact, it was all too familiar. She dropped her head to the ground and closed her eyes. But the feeling grew stronger, engulfed her. And then there was only black-ness.

It was spring and the world was awakening. Creatures large and small were emerging from winter homes, looking to see what the world had in store. The land was awakening from its winter rest, busy with the freshness of new life. The tall pine and oak trees swayed in the gentle breeze. The air was warm but it would be cold tonight, the scent of winter still in the air. Some grasses and bushes low to the ground were showing faint signs of green, foretelling the begin-nings of life in the forest.

Shinaka lay motionless as the waves of despair, discomfort, and disorientation swept over her. She was certain the feeling would pass, but how long it would take was quite another matter. She had to keep moving. But how? At length, exhaustion wrapped its cloak about her and she slept.

These spells, these episodes of disorientation and general unease, were happening more often. But as the young bird lay motionless, nearly dead to the world, she was beyond thinking, beyond reason.

A vision came and went, much too fleeting to be remembered. And that was a pity. For it held the key, the answer to what was happening to her.

The day broke bright and clear, the air a little cool, but good enough. Shinaka awoke. She was perched in the high branches of a tall tree. Her head was clear and her eyesight keen. She had a vague recollection that the strange feeling had come over her yesterday. It was always this way when she awoke after one of the spells. She stretched her wings out wide and moved them about. She felt strong and ready to hunt.

A movement in the grass drew her attention, and she watched and waited, silent and motionless. The small animal moved cautiously among the bushes and tall grass, always alert for snakes and birds of prey. Seeing none, it hopped onto a rock to get some warmth from the morning sun.

Without a sound Shinaka sprang from the branch and spread her wings. She circled slowly until she was

behind and far above the small animal. It was over in a few seconds. Shinaka tucked in her wings and dove at the unsuspecting creature on the rock. One moment, the little animal was sunning itself near the ground; in the next, it was being carried high into the trees, its life drained by the sharp talons that pierced its furry skin.

It was a scene that was played and replayed many times every day. And life in the forest went on.

"But that little animal!" cried Smiling Fawn. "That is very sad, and now I am very sad."

"Well, it is but a legend, little one," said Brave Wolf. "And in a legend there can be bad things as well as good."

"But it happened so fast," said Smiling Fawn. Deep furrows lined her face.

Brave Wolf said, "I think someone who has been in the world for eight years—someone like you—would understand that such things happen. Even in real life."

"Yes, Grandfather," she said. "I understand, but it still makes me feel sad."

"I will try to tell the story with many happy events, if that is what you want," said Brave Wolf.

"Please go on, Grandfather," said the girl. "I want to hear all of it." With that, the frown left her face; she moved closer to her grandfather and watched as he continued.

Shinaka was young, only one year out of the nest. She had been one of two hatchlings that her mother and

father had nurtured in the large nest of twigs, moss, and soft leaves high in the trees. The other young bird, a male, had failed to survive the first month of his life. He ventured too close to the edge of the nest before he could fly. Their parents had told them over and over again to stay *in* the nest, not *on* the nest. They told the two young birds about other young hawks who were too eager, who had fallen from their nests and had been set upon by snakes or other birds.

And that is what happened to her brother. He stood proudly on the edge of the nest, flapping his wings, showing Shinaka how strong he was. And then he was gone, over the side and onto the ground below. He had cried out for his parents, but his high-pitched voice only made it easier for an adult golden eagle to find him and take him away.

When Shinaka was finished with the small animal, she found herself thirsty and in need of cleaning, for her head and feet were tinged with red. A short flight took her to a small cove of a nearby lake where the water was cool and clear. As Shinaka settled on a low branch, a group of ground squirrels—all alert to the dangers of the forest—hurried away from the lake and into the dense brush that lined the shore. Shinaka watched for a while, making sure she would have the cove all to herself. She wanted to drink and perhaps splash her wings in the shallow water. She felt a few lice scurrying under her wings. They had found a home as she slept on the ground last night.

Yesterday's episode was coming back to her, clearer than any before. In earlier spells, she had a vague recollection of sounds, a voice perhaps. Now she remembered clearly, as if it were happening this minute, that there was a voice and an image.

"I have important things for you to do," the voice had said. It had come from somewhere close behind her. Yes, she had been lying on the ground, unable to move, seeing only green and gray, and then the voice . . . and there had been more. An image! She shook her head and picked at a burr on her left wing. She wasn't sure . . . but she *was* sure. Shinaka knew that she had heard that same voice, those same words, before when the world went all gray and green.

As she splashed in the water, Shinaka rolled these thoughts over in her mind. Again and again she remembered last night, and each time the voice seemed louder, clearer, more urgent. But who owned the voice? What were these important things?

At length, the young hawk flew to a dead oak tree and found a branch close to the smooth, gray trunk. Once settled, she spread her wings to dry. The lice were gone, the burr was gone, and she felt clean once more. Hawks take great pride in their appearance. To be unkempt is like telling the world that you have no self-respect. She gripped the branch as she had been taught and closed her eyes. The recent meal and the warm sun made her sleepy.

"*My granddaughter,*" *said Brave Wolf.* "*Bring me the deerskin bag there by my pipe. Perhaps we can find a way to mend your sleeping mat while I tell the story.*"

Smiling Fawn got to her feet and found the bag. "*I am still angry with the mat, Grandfather,*" *she said.*

"*Yes, little one,*" *he said.* "*But together we may find a way to make it behave.*" *After she was seated, he went on.* "*Now, take the birch needle from the bag, and do it with care. It is sharp . . .*"

"*Ouch!*" *cried Smiling Fawn.* "*I think I have found it.*" *Her face was lit with a wide grin as she handed the bag and the needle to her grandfather.*

"*And now you are playing tricks on an old man,*" *said Brave Wolf.* "*Next time I will send you home, you and your torn mat.*" *He winked and the girl knew he was only teasing.* "*Show me where the mat is torn.*"

She did, and said, "*See, it is very close to the edge, and I cannot get the needle where I want it.*"

Her grandfather said, "*Watch me. I will sew a few stitches, then you can do the rest.*"

Smiling Fawn watched as her grandfather's tanned and leathery fingers guided a length of woolen thread through the eye of the wooden needle. Carefully, he made three stitches in the mat. She smiled at him. "*You are a very good mender, Grandfather. Maybe you could . . .*"

"*No, no,*" *he interrupted.* "*I have shown you. Now you finish. A lesson once learned must be used if we are to keep the knowledge. Here.*" *And he handed the mat and the threaded needle to Smiling Fawn.*

As she held the mat and the needle firmly in her small hands, Brave Wolf went on.

Crash!

The sound was close by, and it roused Shinaka in an instant. One moment she was sleeping peacefully, the next she was wide-awake. The young hawk slowly looked right and left to find the source of the sound. Perhaps a fallen tree or tree branch. She let her head turn until she was looking almost directly behind. But there was nothing to be seen. Quietly, Shinaka moved along the branch toward a neighboring pine tree and into its dense foliage.

Crash!

Again the same unsettling sound, this time closer. Shinaka tipped her head forward and surveyed the ground below. *It is good that I am so high in the tree,* she thought.

The animal she looked down upon was huge, and it was angry. The animal tossed its large brown head from side to side, while flailing at bushes that were in its path. The paws were almost as big as the beast's head with long, black claws that shone in the sunlight.

Then, as if some switch had been thrown, the great animal stood on its hind legs and quietly began eating the blue-black berries of a low-hanging tree.

Shinaka watched with quiet interest as the animal pulled a bunch of berries off the tree with a massive paw. Then, with almost dainty grace, it plucked each

berry and placed it in its mouth. This dining ritual went on for several minutes until the animal's muzzle and paws were covered with the juice of the berries.

Slowly, the animal lowered itself onto its forelegs and then rolled onto the ground. With feet in the air, it licked its paws over and over to clean the last of the juice from its fur. And then it slept.

Shinaka flew to a lower branch to get a closer look at the beast. *A bear of some sort,* she thought. Never before had she seen one so large. She moved to an even lower branch.

"Looking for something, are you?"

Shinaka was startled by the sound. Fear told her to move away to safety. Quickly, she flew to a branch high in the pine tree. She needed to find a safe place, where she could watch and listen without being seen. When she was well hidden among dense branches, she slowly and quietly folded her wings and waited, all her senses attuned to whatever might be near.

"You won't find it there," the voice said. "Not in that tree."

Shinaka realized that it was the same voice that spoke to her when she was dazed and the world turned gray and green. She looked here and there, up and down, in the next tree and the next, even into the sky. But nothing.

For some reason she did not understand, she looked once more at the ground and the sleeping bear. What was she seeing? Did that paw move? It did! It was . . . it was . . . motioning to her . . .

"I don't have all day, Shinaka." The bear wasn't just moving its paw. It was . . . calling to her . . . beckoning her to come closer.

And so she did. The great hawk gathered all her strength and courage and flew down toward the huge bear. Not all at once, mind you, but branch by branch, step by step, until she clung to the lowest branch of the tree.

"You . . . you . . . " she could say no more.

"Go on, Shinaka." The voice was clear, but the great bear was asleep.

"You spoke to me?" asked the hawk.

"Yes," came the simple reply.

"You are the voice I hear when my head swims and I cannot think and the world turns gray and green," said Shinaka. "Who are you?"

"Who am I?" the voice said with a laugh. "Perhaps *what* am I would be more to the point."

"All right," replied Shinaka, "what are you, then?" And she waited.

The voice responded. "First, I am not a bear. This great beast is only a helper, a guide, a symbol. He sleeps and hears nothing of what we are saying. His name is Inik. At my bidding, he has walked for countless days and countless miles in search of you. When you and I have had our little talk, Inik will return to his home, those same countless miles away."

"You . . . whoever or whatever you are . . . you could have come to me," said Shinaka. "You didn't need the bear."

"But I did," said the voice. "You heard my voice before, as you say, when the world turns gray and green. You heard but you did not listen."

"And how can I listen when I am in such a stupor?" she asked.

"That was to get your attention, so you would listen when you were awake, active, alive. The bear, Inik, got your attention, did he not?"

"Most certainly," said Shinaka. "With a crash and another crash, all the flailing. And then eating the berries and washing himself. But the waving paw—that was quite a performance."

"Inik wanted so much to eat all the berries. But I told him if he would do my bidding, he will be home before the mountains are white. It was a good performance wasn't it?" The voice went silent.

"Then what are you?" asked Shinaka.

"I am the spirit of life, one who hopes you and all creatures will live well and prosper. Some call me the Great One and that gives me hope and makes me feel much humility. I have been looking for you since the world was young."

Remembering the voice from earlier days, Shinaka spoke in a quiet measured tone. "You have something for me to do. The voice, your voice said so."

"Yes. I have a task for you, but only if you think you can fulfill my wishes. You must give your self, your heart . . . your *life* to it."

"And what is it that I must give my life to?" asked the hawk.

"There is a valley not far from here that needs you." The voice painted a picture for Shinaka. "It is a green place, where creatures live in peace and harmony. I want very much for it to remain that way. The valley needs a keeper, one who will protect it and its inhabitants. I want you, Shinaka, to be the keeper and protector of the green valley. But you must vow to do it always and forever. Any way you can, life or death."

"But the responsibility sounds so big, so daunting," said Shinaka. "'Anyway I can, life or death.' If I take this on I would have to sacrifice all of what I want to do for the good of the valley."

"Ah," replied the voice with a gentle laugh. "I knew you were the right one. Yes. The keeper and protector of the green valley must set aside all selfish desire. Fulfillment comes as the creatures of the valley prosper. So?" And the voice was silent once more.

Shinaka felt the sun grow warm on her shoulders. Her feathers felt lighter somehow, the grip of her talons stronger, her eyesight keener, and her mind crystal clear. All at once, she felt at peace, completely and utterly at peace.

"Yes," she said finally. "I will be the keeper of the green valley and the protector of all that is there. How will I find it?"

With that, the great bear Inik stirred from his slumber, rose to his feet, and shook off the few leaves and branches that clung to his coat. The sun was directly overhead, and the air was warm. A gentle breeze moved through the trees and bushes, making the branches dance in the sun. Inik growled softly and tossed his head twice showing the way and began to walk. After a moment, Shinaka spread her wings and followed.

"It is finished!" said Smiling Fawn excitedly.

"Yes, little one," said Brave Wolf. "That is the end of the story."

"The sleeping mat, Grandfather." Smiling Fawn held it up proudly. "I finished mending my sleeping mat."

"So you did," said Brave Wolf. "And the story about Shinaka . . ."

"Yes, my grandfather, I heard every word. Tell me, did Shinaka really speak with the Great One?"

"Well," he said, "she spoke to the Great One in the legend. What do you think?"

Smiling Fawn tilted her head to one side as she thought. After a moment, she looked directly at her grandfather, smiled, nodded her head, giggled a little, and said, "I think that is a good story, my grandfather, a very good story."

NULUK

NULUK

I t was a warm summer evening in the village of the Armaha. Brother Sun had filled the sky with light and heat for many days. The rain, so plentiful when spring came to the valley, had ended just after the crops were planted in the village garden. Sister Moon had shown her face two times since rain last fell on the garden. The soil, once dark and moist, had turned gray and crumbly. Without water, the crops in the garden would be lost. It was the duty of the younger members of the tribe to carry water from the river and to pour it on Mother Earth so the plants would survive in the withering heat.

Now in the ninth year of her life, Smiling Fawn was one of the young people who did the watering. Soon after the morning meal each day, she picked up her small wooden bucket and made countless trips between the river and the garden to pour water carefully on the rows of corn. When Brother Sun was high in the sky, she stopped a short time—for a meal of bread and fruit, and then a short rest. Only when the last of Brother Sun had dropped below the trees could she and the others return to their lodges to be with their families.

This evening, after Smiling Fawn and her parents had finished their meal, they heard a voice outside their lodge.

"Strong Wolf, may I visit with you and your family?" It was the voice of Brave Wolf, father of Strong Wolf and grandfather of Smiling Fawn.

The young girl didn't wait for her father to answer. "Yes. Yes. Please come into the lodge, Grandfather." She rose to her feet quickly and went to the door to see her best friend.

"Smiling Fawn," her mother, White Sparrow, said sharply. "Brave Wolf has spoken to your father, not to you." The woman motioned for her daughter to return to her mat.

As Brave Wolf entered, Smiling Fawn sat with legs and arms crossed, her head bowed.

Brave Wolf greeted White Sparrow and Strong Wolf, giving each a warm embrace, and then turned to his granddaughter. In a quiet but stern voice he said, "I am pleased you are happy to see me, little one. But who is the head of this family? Who should speak for the family first?" He waited as Smiling Fawn considered the questions.

"My father, Strong Wolf, is the head of my family and the one who should speak first," said Smiling Fawn. She was looking at the floor and pulling at her fingers nervously. Her mother took Smiling Fawn's hands in hers and the nervous pulling ceased.

Brave Wolf continued: "And who would answer if your father were not here?"

"*My mother, White Sparrow, would answer,*" *said the young girl, still looking down.*

"*Yes,*" *said Brave Wolf. With a lighter tone in his voice, he went on.* "*Perhaps you will raise your eyes from the floor and look at me so I may see your beautiful smile.*"

The girl did so.

"*There,*" *said her grandfather.* "*That is better. Would you like to sit with me a while? There is a fine, gentle breeze tonight, and the stars will shine clearly. Perhaps my little one would like to hear a story.*"

"*Yes,*" *said the girl as she rose to her feet.* "*I would like to hear a story.*" *Then she ran the few steps to her grandfather and threw her arms around his waist.* "*I am sorry, Grandfather,*" *she said quietly.* "*I will try very hard to remember my place.*" *Then to her mother and father:* "*I am sorry I spoke before my father. I will do better . . .*" *She could not finish as tears had filled her eyes.*

Strong Wolf held out his hands to his daughter, and Smiling Fawn put her hands in his and looked directly in his eyes.

After a moment, he said, "*You are young, my daughter. But you and I know that you understand the ways of the Armaha.*" *She nodded and he continued.* "*You must remember that when great joy comes to fill your heart and mind, when you feel you must speak, we can see it in your eyes, my daughter. We need not hear it in your voice. Your father reminds you only because you are so precious to him.*"

39

Strong Wolf raised his head the slightest bit, asking if she understood. Smiling Fawn nodded silently and smiled at her father.

Gently, White Sparrow said to her daughter, "Go with your grandfather. Listen to his story, and forget what you have done. The Great One and Umaqua will not remember — not ever."

Smiling Fawn nodded to her mother that she understood. She took her grandfather's hand and they walked out of the lodge into the evening, illuminated only by a pink and blue sky. They walked along the wide central path of the village, which gave them a clear view of Umaqua. They passed three or four lodges and spoke briefly to others who were enjoying the perfect summer evening. At the end of the path, Smiling Fawn and her grandfather found a quiet place by the edge of the forest.

"Here," said Brave Wolf. "Let us sit on the ground."

They seated themselves beneath a towering oak tree and leaned against the trunk.

When they were settled, Brave Wolf asked, "Do you remember the story of the great hawk?"

"You mean Shinaka?" said Smiling Fawn.

"Yes," he said. "That is the one. And she met a little friend, a hummingbird."

"That was Nuluk," she replied.

"Good," said her grandfather. "There is a story about Nuluk. My father, Gray Wolf, told it to me when I was a young boy. Perhaps you would like to hear it."

"Yes, I would," said Smiling Fawn. She sat with her hands and chin on her knees and looked at her grandfather.

He thought for a moment and began . . .

There it was, that sound again. It was close by but sounded far away. It was dark and he felt wet. He tried to move his head, but something held him fast, something solid. He tried again and he heard a *click*. His beak had touched that solid something, yet he had moved but a little. And he wanted to move again; it was something he *had* to do. Again, there were sounds, this time all around him, but still in that faraway place. He could hear them all, a little muted, a little muffled, but he could hear them just the same.

He moved his head and heard the clicking sound again. *Out,* he thought. *I have to get out. I'm not sure why, but I know I must try.* So he pushed his head up against the solid something that made the clicking sound and heard *crack*—not a big sound like a branch breaking underfoot, but a cracking sound all the same. He pushed again and felt his beak move up and, what? Something strange brushed against his beak. It was soft and wet and smelled like him. And now the sounds were clearer, not so muffled. There were lots of sounds: scraping, scratching, crackling, peeping. He pushed harder with his beak and his head was against that damp body and he knocked his beak at that solid something that was keeping him from being "out." The words sounded again and again in his head: *I have to get out.*

For some reason, he pushed with his right foot, and the solid thing was no more. He could move: head, feet, even his tiny wings. But they were wet and oh so heavy. This certainly was a crowded place, a tangle of damp bodies and feet and heads. And the noise! It was so loud he almost wished he had not come "out."

He tried opening one eye, but the brightness forced him to close it. After a while, he tried again and this time kept both eyes open.

He was one of two very small beings in a nest about the size of a walnut shell. It was made of grass and lichen, and lined with tiny feathers and moss. The other being was as small as he, but it made so much noise he thought there were more in the nest. It didn't take him much time at all to understand that if he made noise, another larger being would come to him and feed him. In time, he would learn this was his mother. He opened his beak and pushed air from inside his tiny body. "Eek! Eek! Eek!" he screamed over and over, adding to the noise.

As the day went along, his body dried, and he was able to move his tiny wings just a bit. His mother spent most of her time sitting on him and the other small being in the nest. Every so often, she would leave for a short time. When she came back, she stuck her long, slender beak in his short, stubby beak and put something there that tasted good. In a few weeks, he would learn to hunt for those same

insects, spiders, and nectar. But for now, he was dependent on his mother to bring food to him.

The brightness that was all around him when he had emerged from the egg was gone. He could see only a soft glow around him. And all the noises he had heard earlier were softening, fading. It was that time of day when Brother Sun sails off behind the great Umaqua, turning the sky deep shades of red, purple, and lilac as he completes his journey. Then there was no light at all. Just before his mother settled over him and his sister, he saw little points of light shining in the night sky and a sliver of Sister Moon as she first appeared. And then he slept.

In a week or so, he noticed small feathers growing on his body. His mother showed him how to clean them, to keep them free of dirt and lice. His sister was growing feathers, too, and their mother spent more time away from the nest. That truly was a relief, for who would wish to be sat on all day long?

One week after that, on a bright, warm morning, his mother spoke to him. "You are growing into a fine little bird. It is time you had a name. Nuluk. You will be called Nuluk, and that is how all the other hummingbirds will know you."

"Hummingbirds?" asked Nuluk. "What are hummingbirds?"

"Why, we all are!" his mother exclaimed. "We and all the small, bright green creatures that live near us are hummingbirds. Now, what is your name?"

"Nuluk," he said. Then he went on slowly and carefully. "My name is Nuluk. That is how all the other hummingbirds will know me." He thought for a moment, then asked, "Does my sister have a name?"

"I am Rega," said the little girl bird with great pride in her voice. "Mother gave me my name yesterday. I am older than you." Then she flapped her little wings, tossed her head back, and found a place to lie down on the other side of the nest.

Quickly, the two young birds grew larger and stronger. The soft, downy gray feathers of a hatchling had been replaced by feathers that were sturdy and green. And their stubby, short beaks became long and narrow as a needle. As they grew, their mother had to feed them more often. It seemed that is all she did. For a day or two, the young birds stood in the nest and flapped their wings. Then they were on the edge of the nest spreading their wings, testing them. Rega was the first to fly. She stood on the nest flapping her wings so hard they made a buzzing sound. In the next instant, she had half-flown and half-hopped to a nearby branch. She looked at her brother still in the nest.

"Oh, Nuluk!" she said with excitement in her voice. "You must try to fly, just like I did. Come out of the nest."

Nuluk wasn't sure he wanted to. "Maybe another time, Rega. I . . . I . . . am not strong enough." But he

flapped his wings trying to make that buzzing sound.

Their mother came to feed them and saw Rega out of the nest. She encouraged her son. "It is time, Nuluk."

He stood on the edge of the nest and beat his wings as fast as he could. Before he knew what was happening, he had flown to a branch near his sister. "Oh!" he said with great surprise. "I *can* fly."

For the next four days, Nuluk and Rega spent most of their time on branches near the nest. When they weren't perched on a branch, they were flying in and around the tree, but never far from the nest, for that is where their mother came to feed them.

On the fifth day, the two young hummingbirds flew from their nest for the last time, for they would never see their mother again and would never return to this nest. They were alone now, flying in opposite directions, each looking to make a life of their own. In human terms, that sounds sad. But for a hummingbird it is the way the Great One has designed for them.

"Grandfather," said Smiling Fawn. "Why are you telling me sad things?"

"Sad things?" replied Brave Wolf. "I am only telling you the story of Nuluk."

"I know," said the young girl. "But Rega has gone one way and Nuluk another. Will they ever see each other again?" Smiling Fawn's face was worried, and she frowned.

Brave Wolf chose his words carefully. "In life, we may meet someone and know them for a time. After that time, they leave us to see other things, other people, other places. And sometimes it is we who leave to explore, to learn more of Mother Earth."

"But Nuluk is so small," said the young girl.

"I see," he said, beginning to understand. "You are small and that worries you. It is different with birds and animals, little one. They leave the den or the nest very early. It is the way of the Great One. Now, may I go on?"

Smiling Fawn nodded and moved closer to her grandfather. The breeze had freshened, and the air was cooler now.

Nuluk flew to a branch high up in a tall tree; it was an ancient pine. He wanted to see all there was around him before deciding which way to go. He saw a wide ribbon of water, a river. He flew to it and followed it as it made its way slowly between fields of grass and small bushes.

Feeling adventurous, Nuluk flew across the river and perched on a low bush with red flowers dancing in the breeze. He hovered by them and lowered his long, slender bill into each blossom. The nectar was cool and sweet. He worked his way along the river, darting from one bush to the next, drinking his fill of nectar. That and a few small spiders made a fine meal.

As Brother Sun left the sky, Nuluk found a perch in a sycamore and there he spent his first night out of the nest. With the faint light of evening fading into darkness, he thought of his mother and Rega and the nest in the thorny apple tree where he first saw the world. He watched through sleepy eyes as Sister Moon rose in the sky. At last, Nuluk slept, and he dreamed of what might be somewhere along the river or beyond the rolling hills where Brother Sun had gone.

The next morning, Nuluk decided to learn more about the river. It seemed to be a never-ending source of adventure for the young hummingbird. At first, the water flowed slowly and evenly, its surface reflecting the light and the warmth of Brother Sun.

After it passed by the largest rock Nuluk had ever seen, the river narrowed, and the water became rough and frothy. It tumbled over and around rocks, some just beneath the surface, others that jutted far out of the water.

Nuluk hovered over the beating, bashing water for a moment and thought the river had disappeared. He flew up into a tall tree and looked down. Instead of flowing across the land, the river seemed to pour itself straight down into what seemed like a deep hole, ending in a great cloud of mist. Nuluk could hear the roar of the falls, water crashing against rocks, and more water below. It was dangerous and thrilling at the same time, and the young bird wanted to see it close at hand.

He flew away from the cataract until the river flowed smoothly once again. A closer look showed him that the water moved quickly in the lower streambed. Nuluk found a branch on a small bush on the edge of the river near the base of the falls. He was sure the waterfall was as tall as a mountain. He watched as a flying ant of some sort landed nearby. Nuluk eyed it for a moment or two, and then it disappeared into his beak.

The river widened once more and slowed, flowing in an unhurried manner until it emptied itself into what Nuluk thought must be an endless body of water. For as far as he could see, even from the top of the tallest pine tree he could find, the

water had no end. *It would be foolish to fly for too long a distance above that water,* he thought. At the same time, he felt a strange pull, an urge to fly as far as he could over that water. And in time, he would.

Nuluk hopped into the air and hovered for a moment, looking at the river and the enormous expanse of water below, wanting to remember this place so he could return. With a sense of peace and happiness, he turned to where Brother Sun goes to rest and began to fly. His good brother shone brightly and it was easy to see the land in front of him. The little bird flew until the day was almost spent, then he found a dense bush and settled there among its protective covering for the night. Of course, he had stopped for nectar from the colorful flowers he found along the way. Before closing his eyes, his last thought was of a flower with particularly sweet nectar. It was purple . . . or blue . . . or violet . . . or . . . But sleep took hold, and he never did finish that thought.

In two days' time, Nuluk found himself in a valley surrounded at the foot of a mountain. He explored the entire valley, the small streams that flowed there, the stands of trees that dotted the valley. And on the fourth day in this new place, he saw others that looked and sounded like him, a great flock of hummingbirds. Nuluk was adventurous, but he was shy, not one to go out of his way to meet other animals, and certainly not other hummingbirds. He kept his distance, waiting for the right moment. Or that's what he told himself.

"Grandfather," said Smiling Fawn excitedly. "He came to our valley. Is that right?"

"Well, the story does not tell us," said the old man. "But there is more to the story. Or should we finish it another time?"

"No, no, Grandfather," said the girl. "Please finish it now."

Suddenly, the air was filled with a bright flash of light and it seemed for a moment as if Brother Sun had returned. Seconds later, the quiet night was consumed with a clap of thunder so loud and so near that Smiling Fawn and Brave Wolf could feel it in the ground where they sat.

With eyes wide and hope in her voice, the girl said, "Thunder! Lightning! Grandfather, does that mean rain?"

"It might mean rain will come," he replied in an even voice. "Or it could be nothing more than a flash of light and a loud noise. We must wait for Mother Earth and the Great One to decide such things. But let us finish the story. You need your sleep so you can tend the corn tomorrow."

"Yes, I know," sighed the girl. "I would like to hear you tell the story."

"Let us see," said Brave Wolf. "Nuluk was . . ."

"Nuluk has just seen a flock of hummingbirds, Grandfather," said Smiling Fawn. "But he wants to wait a while before he speaks to them."

"Yes," said Brave Wolf. "Now I remember."

Nuluk was startled by a voice speaking to him—a voice very near to him.

"And how long were you going to be in our midst without so much as a simple greeting?"

Nuluk almost fell to the ground when he heard the voice. He had been sipping from a flower with deep red petals, lost in the business of enjoying his nectar. "I . . . uh . . . I . . . uh . . . I must go." It was all he could think to say.

"Go?" said the other hummingbird with a little laugh. "And where would that be?" He waited for an answer.

Nuluk gathered himself. "To my new home," he said nervously. "That is it. I must go to my new home." Surely that would satisfy his questioner.

The other bird spread his wings and raised his long beak, standing as tall as he possibly could. The bright red spot under his chin shone like fire, the mark of an older hummingbird. "Perhaps *this* is your new home, my young master." He waited.

Nuluk had considered this possibility, but shyness made him hesitate. "I . . . I . . . I'll think on it," he said.

"Maybe I'll come by tomorrow," said the other hummingbird. "I am called Sarak, and I will bring a few friends with me. I would like you to join our flock. We can use an adventurous sort like you." Sarak rose and flew to the other end of the valley where his flock was resting in a row of bushes along one of the streams.

Nuluk turned those last words over and over in his mind. He had never thought of himself as adventurous, only a young hummingbird trying to find his way. Thoughts raced in his head: *And what about these "few friends" that might come with the other bird? Maybe I'll leave this valley today. And why would I do that? He seemed friendly enough.* Then, finally he thought, *I'll stay one more day just to see . . . just to see.*

The next day, as Brother Sun finally appeared through the early morning haze, Nuluk flew to that patch of purple or blue or violet flowers. He was starting to sip nectar from a blossom when he saw and heard the group of birds approaching, and there were more than "a few."

Sarak was leading the others—there must have been a dozen—right toward Nuluk.

"Good morning, friend," said Sarak. "We would like to talk to you." And then added, "If you have the time."

"Yes, yes," said Nuluk. He flew to a nearby pussy-willow bush and wiped his bill back and forth on a catkin. The nectar in that last flower was sweet but a little sticky. He settled himself on a branch in front of the older bird, but a little higher in the bush.

"All right," Sarak replied. "First, we would like to know your name and where you come from."

"I am called Nuluk. I come from a forest in the mountains." He pointed with his bill. "In that direction, where Brother Sun starts his daily journey.

52

I followed a river to the sea or a large lake, and then came here."

Sarak thought for a moment. "You have been to every corner of our valley." Then he added with a wink, "And you have tasted the nectar of our flowers." At that remark, the other birds made little chittering sounds. "Let us remember our manners," Sarak said. And the air was silent once more.

"Very nice flowers," said Nuluk, unable to hide how uneasy he felt.

"Will you join our flock?" It was a small female hummingbird who reminded him of his sister, Rega. But this little bird, cute in her own way, spoke in soft tones, not harsh and teasing like his sister.

Cautiously, Nuluk replied, "I must go to my new home. It is . . . it is something I have to do." And he dropped his head, breaking eye contact with the little female bird.

"My name is Tama," she said. "I would not want to appear to be too bold, but I for one would like you to stay." There was more chittering among the flock, agreeing with Tama. This time the older bird said nothing.

Something stirred inside Nuluk. "I will stay until the next time we see all of Sister Moon in the night sky. Beyond that, I cannot say."

Tama was pleased and chittered something to another female on the branch above her.

All was quiet for a long moment, after which Sarak spoke. "I am the eldest in the flock. I am pleased that you will stay with us for a while." Looking directly at Tama, he continued. "And the *flock* is pleased as you can see and hear." The chittering began anew, and although he was looking at the grass below him, Nuluk could feel Tama's eyes looking directly at him.

"There is something I don't understand," said Smiling Fawn.

"And what is that?" asked Brave Wolf.

"Tama, the girl hummingbird," said Smiling Fawn. "Why was she looking at Nuluk?"

"Let me see," said her grandfather, searching for a good answer. "Perhaps she wanted to be friends with Nuluk. Yes, that is it, she needed a new friend. What do you think?"

"I don't know," said the girl, tilting her head to one side. "I will have to think about that."

Without warning, the breeze suddenly became a gust of wind that rattled the tools that leaned against the lodge and sent a moaning sound through the trees. Brave Wolf and his granddaughter felt the first drops of rain and rose to their feet. As they walked, they could feel the freshening breeze and see the dark clouds moving through the sky. They stopped in front of her lodge.

"Go inside, little one," said Brave Wolf. "I can walk to my lodge alone. You should be inside and away from the rain. Wish your mother and your father well this night. And I pray the Great One watches over you . . . always."

"Thank you, Grandfather," she said. "I will thank the Great One for sending rain. The corn will not need my help tomorrow."

The rain began to fall harder. As her grandfather entered his own lodge, Smiling Fawn turned her face to the sky to let the quenching water dance on her face and into her mouth.

BRAVE WOLF

BRAVE WOLF

When did our people come to this valley?" She was only ten years of age, but Smiling Fawn was an inquisitive child, always wanting to know more about her people.

Her grandfather had come to expect such questions from the young girl and chose his words carefully. "It was many years ago, little one." He hesitated, knowing that any answer he gave would be beyond the child's grasp. "The elders say that before we arrived here, Sister Moon had made her journey across the night sky countless times."

"And Umaqua, was she here when our people arrived?" asked Smiling Fawn.

"Oh, yes." Brave Wolf smiled and laughed at the question. "The mountain we call Umaqua was created long ago by the Great One. And do not ask me how many times Sister Moon has coursed the sky since then. It is enough to know that this valley and all the other valleys and all the streams and other mountains were placed here by the Great One, and long before our people came to the green valley."

The young girl shook her head a little, trying to understand all she had just heard. It was quite confusing.

"When did you come to this valley, Grandfather?" she asked. And with eyes wide open, she waited for the answer.

"So you want to know how Brave Wolf came to the green valley . . ."

"Yes, and how your mother and father chose your name."

Smiling Fawn sat cross-legged facing the tanned and wrinkled face, waiting, for she knew he would think for a few moments before speaking again. She put her elbows on her knees and rested her chin in her hands.

"This is as I remember it," said Brave Wolf. His eyes glistened as he spoke.

My father was called Gray Wolf. His name came from the streak of gray hair on the left side of his head. It was there when he was born. Gray Wolf was a quiet man, a man of great physical strength, a man of great wisdom and kindness. My mother was called Sanchea. It was a strange name for a woman of the Armaha, but you remember she was from another tribe. Only by the hand of the Great One did she and Gray Wolf find each other. It is told that when Gray Wolf took her as his own, the light from Sanchea's smile was an omen that the year ahead would bring peace and abundance to the Armaha.

In time, Sanchea bore a son, Gray Deer. He too had a streak of gray hair, just like Gray Wolf. A year later, I came into the world, and the family was complete: Gray Wolf, Sanchea, Gray Deer, and Brave Wolf.

At that time, the Armaha lived . . ."

"Your name," Smiling Fawn interrupted. "How did you come to be called Brave Wolf? You said you would tell that story, too."

"And so I shall," replied her grandfather. He thought for a moment, then continued.

One day in the first year of my life while learning to walk, I started toward my father on unsteady legs, and I fell. Not a hard fall. I lost my balance and sat on the ground. My father was watching, and when I realized he was there, I sobbed like a stricken child. He knew I wasn't hurt, and let me blubber for a moment. Then he simply put one finger to his mouth, telling me to be silent. I stopped crying and, holding on to a large pot, I stood up. Once again, I began walking, and once again, I lost my balance and sat on the ground. This time I looked at my father. He watched me and motioned for me to get up. I repeated the dance of getting up, losing my balance, and sitting down several more times, but I had forgotten about crying. When I had made my way to my father's feet, he held out his hand to me. I grasped one finger, and he lifted me safely into his arms.

He laughed as only my father could laugh, and called to my mother. "Sanchea, I have chosen a good name for our second son. We will call him Brave Wolf."

"And that is how I came to be called Brave Wolf. May I go on with the other story now?"

"Yes, Grandfather, please go on."

"At that time the Armaha lived . . ." said Brave Wolf.

"Yes, Grandfather?" asked Smiling Fawn. She watched as he frowned a little, looking to his left and right. Softly she said, "Your family was complete."

"Ah yes," he replied. "Now I remember."

Smiling Fawn smoothed the deerskin cloak over her crossed knees and waited.

At that time, the Armaha lived on the other side of Umaqua, where Brother Sun goes at the end of each day. The high valleys were pleasant and bountiful. The grass was lush and thick, so good for our horses, and also good for the animals we hunted. They were plentiful and always of good size. An unending flow of water coursed down from Umaqua. But when the snow came, living became difficult. Even with extra skins to wear, we were cold all the time.

A hunting party that had climbed to the other side of the mountain returned with stories of a broad valley. "Where the morning sun shines on Umaqua," they said. Their story was so wonderful that a larger group of men was sent to hunt in this new place to see these wonders for themselves. When they returned, their descriptions were just as others had told earlier. Not long after, the council decided that all of the Armaha would make a new home on the other side of Umaqua.

There was much discussion about leaving the place the Armaha called home. Some thought this would displease the Great One and would bring great suffering to the tribe. Others wanted to stay near the sacred place where those who had gone on before were buried. But the council had decided, and the Armaha would go to make a new home. From that day on, all our energy was devoted to preparing for the trek to the other side of Umaqua.

As soon as the rainy season ended, four families started the journey. They followed the path the first hunters had taken, about halfway up Umaqua then around the side of the mountain. Once on the other side, they would have to make their own trail into the valley, or follow paths worn by animals.

A few days later another group started out, this time following the stream that flowed along the base of Umaqua. The next group to leave took the mountain trail; the group after that followed the stream.

Before our family was to leave, Gray Deer became ill. My brother and I were in the sixth and fifth years of our lives and seemed to be strong little boys. But Gray Deer awoke one day with a fever and a cough. Sanchea and the other women of the tribe used all their knowledge, but nothing would ease Gray Deer's troubles. He was immersed in the cold waters of a mountain stream. Surely, that would bring relief. But his fever seemed to strengthen. Roots and herbs were gathered to make a strong broth, but that failed also.

Our family was to be in the last group to make the journey to our new home. But Gray Deer was far too weak to travel, and so we would stay behind for a few days.

Sanchea and Gray Wolf were good people, strong people. It seemed they could conquer anything and anyone. But they could not conquer this thing that had consumed Gray Deer. One day after we had waved to that other group and wished them well, Gray Deer went to live with the Great One. Gray Wolf was deeply saddened, but would shed not one tear. That was forbidden. Sanchea cried softly for most of the day, remaining inside our wood and mud home.

As Brother Sun began to leave the sky, Gray Deer's body was taken to the sacred grounds and placed in a suitable grave. When the dirt and rocks had been placed, Gray Wolf raised his hands to the darkening sky and recited the words that had been taught through the ages:

> The strength of our people is only through your strength.
>
> Even in our sorrow, we look to you, Great One, for peace and wisdom.
>
> Here now, this boy, Gray Deer, returns to you.
>
> He is the greatest gift we can give, for his is a strong and true heart.

"Grandfather, what you tell me has brought tears to my eyes. I do not want to hear more." Smiling Fawn wiped the edges of her moist brown eyes.

"Life is not always happy, little one. Last year you remember that your father, Strong Wolf, released his favorite horse—one he had raised from birth—and sent it off to find a final resting place. That is a part of the way the world moves on. I do not understand all of it. Perhaps one day the Great One will explain it to us." Smiling Fawn nodded; her eyes were clear now. "Let me tell more of the story. I will make sure I tell only of the happy days." He looked at the precious child out of the corner of his eye.

"It is all right, Grandfather," she said, a smile returning to her face. "You can tell of sad things . . . but not too many."

"Yes. I understand." He squeezed her hands gently and returned to his story.

The journey to our new home was not an easy one. We started the next morning, climbing up the side of Umaqua. The path was well marked and not so steep. Our three horses carried most of the things we needed for the new home. Sanchea, Gray Wolf, and I each carried a small bundle of food.

As Brother Sun reached the top of his daily journey and was directly overhead, we found ourselves on the path leading around Umaqua. We stopped and looked back at the high valley that had been our home. It was a sad moment. Sanchea closed her eyes and murmured a few words to herself. All I could hear was a name, Gray Deer. She was saying good-bye once more. My father nodded his head as if echoing Sanchea's thoughts. Soon we came to the trail that led around the mountain and into the valley that would be our new home. It would take two more days just to walk and climb around Umaqua. The trail had been marked by those who had gone earlier, but parts of it were rough or slippery, and a misstep could mean a broken bone or even something much worse.

"Grandfather!" exclaimed Smiling Fawn. "You said you would tell good things and not so many of the bad things."

"I thought I had chosen my words carefully, Granddaughter," replied the old man. "The trail around Umaqua is a dangerous one. I would not want you to know anything less." And he waited.

Smiling Fawn looked at her hands for a moment, turning them this way and that. It is what she did sometimes when she was thinking. And then she spoke. "Yes. I understand. Tell me, what is the first thing you remember about our valley? When you saw it for the first time, what did you think?"

He replied, "The next part of the story will answer your questions, little one."

After another four days—that makes seven in all—we had climbed down to the floor of the valley. On the last day of the descent, I marveled at the size of it, for it seemed to go on forever. That's what I thought, anyway. And it was so green. But there was something more—a feeling perhaps, a sense that it was a good place, a peaceful place.

Our journey to the new valley took longer than we had planned, two days longer. Just as we made our way to this side of Umaqua, we were faced with a rainstorm. We had been expecting rain for a few days; the air was heavy and the scent of rain was everywhere. As we started down into the valley, it came upon us. Wind howling in the trees and rain driving right at us. It is good that we were off the mountain. If we had been on the rocky trail . . . Well, we were far away from it and that was good.

Our horses were tired and the sudden storm had them nervous, scared. A flash of lightning made us all jump. Mother and I cried out. Gray Wolf said nothing; he kept leading us on in the face of the storm. The only protection we could find was under the branches of a young pine tree. Another flash of lightning was followed by a cracking sound I had never heard before. A large tree not too far in front of us was in flames and falling to the ground. It fell in our direction, but landed a good distance away. The fire was quenched by the driving rain, but the broken, smoldering hulk smoked, steamed, and hissed as if it were some monster waiting for us, daring us to walk in its direction. We huddled close together with the three horses. Gray Wolf held their leads tight in his hand. Sanchea took two large skins from the packs that were slung on the animals and draped them over the three of us. The horses braved the rain as best they could.

During the night, we saw more lightning and heard more thunder, some seemed to be right over our heads. The excitement of the storm and the difficulties of our journey got the better of me, and I slept a few hours. I am sure my parents kept watch all night without sleeping. When I awoke, the rain had softened to almost nothing and the sky showed signs of clearing. My mother and father were busily loading the skins on the horses. After eating a bit of dried meat, we set out to find the rest of our tribe.

The village was only a collection of temporary shelters, but the faces of the people made it feel like home. We were tired and wet and not the cleanest members of the tribe. But surely, we were the happiest. I saw a friend, Red Eagle, a boy my own age. We smiled at each other and waved a greeting.

Then there was silence. The chief and his wife came to my parents and asked about Gray Deer. The people gathered near to hear the answer. It was too much for Sanchea. She put a hand to her eyes, and two other women put their arms around her and led her away. My father told of Gray Deer's death and his burial. I remember hearing words meant to help, and I remember hearing a few sobs among the people. Red Eagle put his hands on my shoulders and looked into my eyes. Without a word, he was telling me to be strong. Then he squeezed my shoulders and walked away. He and I would never ever speak of Gray Deer again. It is the way of our people. Once a man or a woman, or a boy or a girl, is given back to the Great One, we keep them in our heart.

In a few days, we had built our own shelter. All our people began the work of making the valley our home. A few weeks later, just as Brother Sun was leaving the sky, two or three of our elders gathered near the large fireplace in the middle of our temporary village. They started singing one of the songs they learned as boys and young men. It told of a great hunt when much meat was taken to feed our people for the cold months.

These brave men climbed on our friend Umaqua.

They found the path to hunt and to find a true life.

They pleased the Great One,

And they were given a gift.

69

With a note of sorrow in his voice, Brave Wolf said to Smiling Fawn, "I suppose the story in that song is not so different from the trek our people made from the high valley where Gray Deer is buried to this green valley where we live today." He went on in a happier voice: "And tomorrow when Sister Moon rides high in the night sky, you will hear that song. Do you like that story, little one?"

"Yes, Grandfather," she replied. "Although it is touched with sadness, it is a story filled with hope. And I like that very much."

UMAQUA

UMAQUA

The river swirled and danced among the rocks, sounding like some ancient beast growling at the world. Brother Sun shone bright and warm, making the large rocks along the bank a good place to sit and enjoy a summer afternoon. Chores of the day had been finished before the noon meal, and now it was time to do other things.

Brave Wolf held Smiling Fawn's hand as they walked toward the rushing stream. He said, "You asked me to tell you the story of how Umaqua came to be. Are you sure you want to hear the story again?"

They found their favorite rock—one shaped like a large basket—and settled themselves.

"Yes, Grandfather," she responded hopefully. "You said you would tell me on the first day of the next year of my life. And that is today."

"And so I will." His eyes shone with mischief. "Now, where will I begin?"

"Oh, Grandfather," the young girl said, losing patience. "You always say that!"

"And what do you say when I ask that question?" He waited as Smiling Fawn sat very still, her head tilted to one side thinking how to answer.

"I always say, 'Just start at the beginning.' But you know that, so please, please tell me the story."

Brave Wolf smiled and nodded. "It is a long story, covering even the time before there was time. But I will shorten it."

Smiling Fawn was concerned. "Are you going to leave anything out of the story?"

"No, little one," he said. "I will not leave anything out. Now, make yourself comfortable."

Smiling Fawn pulled absently at the two braids her mother had woven with her long, black hair. She smoothed them on the front of her cloak and waited.

Long ago, before our people came to this land, even before we found the valley on the other side of Umaqua, things looked quite different. Legends tell us that at one time ice and snow covered all of what we see today. Stories told by three fathers before my father, Gray Wolf, remind us of a time when our world was much different. This may be hard to believe, but in times past, the mountain we call Umaqua, our Sacred House, did not stand where she stands today.

There was a man—tall, lean, aged—who roamed over the world as it was. In the legend, he is called Ahote, the Restless One. The deep lines in his

forehead and the crow's feet at the corners of his eyes were reminders of long days spent in the glare of Brother Sun. His eyes were the color of a summer night, deep and dark and, at the same time, sparkling. His hair was long and dark, streaked here and there with silver; it fell almost to his waist. He tied it with a leather thong adorned with a nugget of silver he had found along a creek bed. His skin was tanned and leathery. The fingers on Ahote's hands were long and slender, capable of delicate, careful work. And yet his hands were firm and strong, ready for climbing, for lifting, for dealing with the realities of life. He wore a shirt and trousers of deerskin, decorated only with ancient symbols of life, fire, wind, and rain. On his feet, he wore short buckskin boots. The broad-brimmed hat that sat upon his head was made from a hide of some sort; he adorned it with a thin leather thong and a single white feather taken from an eagle's nest. The trace of a smile was always on his face, for he believed that happiness was a cure for the loneliness he endured.

The world was mostly flat with few mountains or hills. Brother Sun shone bright and hot. So hot that sometimes Ahote moved about only after Brother Sun went to sleep each night or when the clouds hid Brother Sun. It was a lonely life for Ahote, for he lived without family or friends.

One morning when Sister Moon had finished her journey, Ahote awoke and spied something shining in the distance. It would sparkle for just a moment, then seem to disappear from sight. It was much too far away for him to see the object clearly, but he felt a need to go to it. Even before Brother Sun appeared that day, Ahote placed a large flat rock over the fire that had kept him warm through many nights, and began walking. He faced where Brother Sun goes to rest, keeping his eyes on the place where the shining object was.

He walked one day, then two days, then three. On the third day of his journey, he found a small pond of sweet water. He drank his fill and waited there hoping an animal might stop for a drink and become a meal for him. He waited most of that day and part of the next. Finally, a small rabbit hopped into view. He had wanted more, but the small animal would have to do. There was no meat left for another meal.

Ahote stood on a small boulder and looked to see the shining object in the distance. There it was, but it seemed he wasn't any closer to it. That made him wonder, but having spied the object, he started off once again. Three more days he walked, this time stopping beside a fast-flowing stream. As he approached, he could see large fish jumping in the water. Ahote fashioned a sharp stick from a tree branch and waded into the stream. If a fish came near, he would have another meal. All day his stomach had reminded him that it was empty and in need of food. In less time than you can say Sister Moon, he had speared two of the large fish. As he had done with the rabbit, Ahote cooked the fish over a fire he started with two magic stones he carried in a small sack around his neck.

"But they are not magic stones, Grandfather. We use them all the time to make a fire for cooking." Smiling Fawn *always questioned what she thought was untrue.*

"Yes, little one, the stones are not magic today. But the story would not be very interesting without such things."

"What about Umaqua, Grandfather?" She said impatiently.

"If you will listen, I will get to that. Now where was I?" He waited for Smiling Fawn to remind him.

She didn't disappoint him. *"Ahote has cooked two large fish, and . . ."*

"Yes. I remember now," said Brave Wolf.

Ahote made four meals of the fish. One he ate that day; the rest he saved for the journey ahead. Looking from atop another boulder, he saw the shining object and started out in its direction. As he walked, he thought, *Seven times Brother Sun has made his way across the sky, and still I am no closer to the shining object. Perhaps I am mistaken. Perhaps I am only chasing a dream.*

But on he walked, believing he would soon find whatever was out there drawing him onward, calling to his heart. The journey would consume the rest of one year and most of the next. Ahote saw rivers as wide as three meadows and a desert that burned his feet during the day and chilled him through and through at night. He crossed hundreds of animal paths, using them to find game so he could eat. He

saw birds and animals he had never seen before: great antlered animals that ran like the wind and herds of long-tusked, hairy beasts that huddled close together to protect their young when the winter wind blew. In the middle of the second year, he came to a sea that seemed to stretch forever. The surface of the water reflected the color of the sky. The lines of endless waves rolled easily to the sandy shore, making but a small, lapping sound as they reached out to the land. And when Ahote looked far out where Brother Sun ends his daily journey, it seemed the sky and sea melted together.

He remained in this place for some time, exploring the coves, inlets and marshes, and the streams and rivers that flowed into the sea. As time passed and Brother Sun rode low in the sky, the wind grew stronger, bringing cooler air to the land. It was a signal for Ahote to turn away from the water, to seek shelter from the cold that was sure to come. And it was time to resume his search for the shining object that drew him onward.

Some days later Ahote lay sleeping in a small depression covered with dried leaves and branches. The ground was covered in white. Snow and wind had been howling around him for so many days he had lost count. Sister Moon peeked out from behind a cloud, shining a beam at his right eye. Ahote awoke with a start, sure that some animal was about to pounce on him. He cleared sleep from his eyes and his mind, and he watched as a swirl of wind picked

up a small pile of leaves and scattered them across the snow. The moonbeam that had awakened him moved across the snow to where the leaves had been. Something glistened ever so slightly, just enough for him to see. The snow at his feet and the cold air made him shiver, but his eyes held fast to the glow he could see clearly on the ground. Carefully he walked the five paces to the spot, not wanting to lose sight of whatever was there. On hands and knees, he gently swept the snow away, revealing a small stone. It was no bigger than a hummingbird's egg, but it shimmered and shone as if it were Sister Moon herself. He looked skyward and saw she was once again behind a cloud, but the small stone continued to glow, to shine and shimmer in his hand.

Now standing, he slowly turned the stone over and over in his hands. No matter which way he turned it, the stone shone with a brilliance he had never seen before. A thought came to him: *It seems to shine brighter the longer I hold it, and it is getting warm.* After a moment or two another thought: *It is hot like fire!* He dropped the small stone. It melted through the snow and lost some of its luster, but continued to shine. Ahote knelt beside the stone and realized he was no longer cold. Snow was all around him, the ground was covered, and an icy wind sang in the nearby trees and bushes. But he was warm. It was as if Brother Sun were shining down halfway through his daily journey.

And then a voice from inside said, "Not here. Take the stone to another place."

Aloud, Ahote asked, "What other place?"

The voice answered, "You must return to the place where your journey began. Wrap the stone in the three softest leaves you can find; keep it hidden as you travel. You must start today, now. Turn to where Brother Sun appears each day . . . and go."

Ahote did as the strange voice commanded. He found leaves of birch, aspen, and alder. From them he selected three that felt soft, almost furry, when he rubbed them against his face. He placed the small stone on the leaf from the birch tree, the softest of the three, and folded it carefully, making sure the stone was completely covered. He wrapped it with the alder leaf, for it came from a strong tree and would protect the small stone. Finally, he covered it with the aspen leaf, its golden color reminding him of summer mornings when the air is clear and the world is awakening.

When he had finished, Ahote stood and faced the place where Brother Sun rises from the land each morning. In the distance, he recognized a row of trees that he had passed two days earlier. From there he would find other landmarks to guide him. He took a deep breath, made sure the packet of leaves was secure in his waistband, and began his new journey.

"Good," said the voice from inside. "When your journey is done, the land will be complete."

Ahote walked to the line of trees without stopping to rest or eat, all the time feeling the warmth of Brother Sun on his neck and shoulders. He sat on the

ground, his back against one of the trees and looked where he had been. The plain that he had walked on just days before was a plain no more. Now his view was interrupted by hills. And beyond the hills, mountains had appeared, as if by magic, all covered with snow, pure white snow. Ahote closed his eyes and shook his head, thinking he was only imagining, but when he opened his eyes, the mountains and hills were still there.

The voice spoke to him. "Yes, Ahote, what you see is real. Rest for the night and continue on tomorrow."

At the end of each day when Ahote turned to look where he had been, he could see that the land was changing. Small streams he crossed had become wide, slow-moving rivers. A pond where he had stopped for a drink had become a vast body of water that seemed to have no boundaries. The voice inside reassured him along the way, encouraging him to continue, reminding him that as he walked the land would change.

"But what made the land change, Grandfather? It was mostly flat, and suddenly there are mountains with snow on top and hills and great rivers and lakes." As many times as Smiling Fawn had heard this story, she had said these things. She was a bright child of eleven years and yet completely taken in by the legend.

Her grandfather thought for a moment, remembering the answer he had given the last time and thinking how to change it. "Perhaps we can think of it this way, little one.

The voice Ahote heard might be that of the Great One. And we know the Great One can do anything. Perhaps Ahote was chosen to assist the Great One to complete the land."

"I don't know, Grandfather," said Smiling Fawn. "I will have to think about that. Now, what does the legend say about Umaqua?"

One day—Ahote had lost count how many—he recognized the place where he had snared the rabbit by the sweet water pond more than three years before. The pond was larger now, more like a small lake. And hills had risen around it where none had been before. Ahote realized he would have to walk around the lake and over these new hills to reach his destination.

The next day, halfway around the lake, Ahote saw the path he had taken to this place sometime before, a path worn by animals over many years. Now it would lead him into the hills and from there he did not know. He would have to follow it and to trust the voice that spoke to him.

After more days on the path, Ahote walked into a small clearing and found a tree to lean against. As he always did, he made sure the packet of leaves was wedged safely beneath his waistband. He took it out and examined it carefully, lovingly turning the small packet over and over in his hands. It was a ritual he had repeated every day of his journey. A small bird landed on a flat rock only a few paces away. Watching the little creature as it chirped its song and bobbed its head, looking this way and that, Ahote felt the place was familiar. And it was. The little bird was standing on the flat rock he had placed over the small stone fireplace.

He arose and with great excitement asked aloud, "Is this the place? Have I found it?"

The voice inside answered: "Yes, my son, you have found the place where your journey began. And you have changed the land. But we are not yet finished."

"Must I walk more?" asked Ahote. He was almost afraid what the answer might be.

The voice: "No. Your walking has come to an end, Ahote. Remove the small stone from the packet of leaves, but carefully. It must not touch the ground . . . not here."

He did as the voice told him. Ahote sat on the ground and carefully unwrapped the packet of leaves, first the golden aspen leaf, then the leaf of the alder tree, still showing its orange and red streaks, and finally, the soft feathery birch leaf. From the last, he took out the small stone and placed it in the palm of his left hand. All the time Ahote held his breath, not sure what might happen. After a moment or two, the stone began to glow, just as it had when he found it beneath the snow.

"Which hand do you use to throw a spear, Ahote?" It was the voice asking a very strange question.

Ahote held up his right hand and said, "This one, this one."

83

"Ahote," said the voice. "Walk to the middle of the clearing and stand, facing where Brother Sun goes to rest. Place the stone in your right hand. And when it becomes so hot you think it will burn your hand, throw it as hard and as far as you can."

"But it is so small, it will not go very far," said Ahote, almost complaining.

The voice answered, "Do not worry, my son. If you trust me, all will be well."

Slowly, Ahote walked to the middle of the small clearing and turned around. He could see the stone was shining more brightly, and he could feel the stone becoming warm, then hot in his hand. He held it with his thumb and two fingers. Then when the heat of the small stone made him cry out, he hurled it as hard as he could.

The small stone flew out of his grasp, soaring far over the trees that surrounded the clearing. Before his right arm was back at his side, Ahote lost sight of the stone. The air was still. The voice was silent. As he had before his journey, Ahote felt alone.

The silence was broken by a booming sound. It was far off in the distance, but the sound was clear to Ahote. The earth trembled beneath his feet, and shook with great force, knocking him down. Ahote reached for a nearby tree and hung on in fear. The shaking and trembling continued. On one side of the clearing the ground was ripped open as if some gigantic hand was breaking a piece of corn bread. Trees and bushes and rocks fell into the gaping rift.

Another violent heaving of the ground and the rift was closed, leaving one side higher. After a few minutes of silence, there was an onrush of air around him that nearly pulled him from the tree. That was followed by excited sounds of birds and animals. Suddenly, a flock of sparrows flew into the trees near the clearing. Quickly, they moved from branch to branch, chattering all the while, then flew off as suddenly as they had come. Animals of all kinds ran into the clearing, charging around him on all sides. The fear in their eyes was plain to see. A large antlered beast with big, brown eyes and a white tail leaped over Ahote. He flattened himself to the ground and covered his head with his hands, afraid he might be kicked or stepped on or gored. A mother fox and her five kits trotted into the clearing, saw Ahote, and stopped. They watched Ahote and sniffed the air, not sure what to do or where to go. A large brown bear, frightened and running close behind the foxes made the choice for them. The foxes jumped over and around Ahote to flee the great brown beast. The bear—wide-eyed and drooling—looked at Ahote for a moment, and then continued his flight of fear, bounding after the foxes. The scene continued until Brother Sun was hidden by the tall trees that circled the clearing. When it was over, Ahote was so exhausted from fear he slept where he had flattened himself on the ground.

In the quiet of the warm summer morning, Ahote awoke, feeling refreshed. The events of yesterday

swam in his head, making him wonder what had happened, what had made the animals and birds so fearful.

"Walk to the other side of the trees, Ahote." It was the voice inside once more. "With your eye, follow the path of the small stone."

He rose and walked as he was instructed. Once beyond the trees, he saw the tallest, most beautiful mountain in the world. The first rays of Brother Sun made something glimmer and shine near the peak of the mountain. Ahote stared at the shining object, knowing he had seen it once before.

"It was the small stone," Smiling Fawn said excitedly. "And the mountain is Umaqua. Is that right, Grandfather?" She was sitting up straight, clapping her hands.

"Yes, the mountain is Umaqua," Brave Wolf replied. "As for the thing that glimmers and shines, I cannot say. You may choose to believe it is Ahote's small stone, my granddaughter. I would like to believe that is so, but one would have to climb high up on our dear Umaqua to find it. And even then, how could you tell. After all . . ."

"Yes, my grandfather, after all Ahote is the only one to hold the stone in his hand . . ."

"And . . ." Brave Wolf prompted the young girl.

"And . . ." Smiling Fawn finished their thought. "The story of Ahote is just a legend."

Brave Wolf held out his arms to Smiling Fawn. "A good story, a good legend, little one?"

The young girl smiled at the old man and threw her arms around his neck. "Yes, Grandfather. You know I like that story." And as she peeked around his head, she could see something glimmering and shining in the snow, high near the top of Umaqua.

THE GREEN VALLEY

THE GREEN VALLEY

I t was a quiet, summer morning, and Smiling Fawn sat
on a small log bench in front of her parent's lodge,
trying to weave a new basket for her treasures. The
strips of willow bark, at once smooth and slippery, made the
task difficult for such a young person. Smiling Fawn scolded
the strips when they refused to obey her small hands and
praised them when they allowed her to move them about.
When finished, the basket would be two hands wide and
three hands deep, a fine place to keep her valuable things.
She had collected a few stones: some smooth, some colorful,
and some with shapes that reminded her of animals. And her
collection of treasures included the jawbone of a small
animal with the teeth all neatly lined up and bleached white
by the sun. There was a single bear's claw on a leather thong
that her grandfather, Brave Wolf, had given to her for good
luck. And, of course, her collection included any number of
bright feathers she had found, the bright orange feather her
favorite.

Smiling Fawn had just finished the bottom of the basket
when she heard someone walking toward the lodge. As she
looked up, a bright smile came over her face. It was her
grandfather, perhaps her closest friend in the world,

although she would never tell anyone. She had one other friend, Standing Lark, a girl about her same age. They had declared themselves to be close friends the last time Sister Moon showed her full face. As these thoughts went through her mind, Smiling Fawn decided it would be a good thing to have more than one close friend.

"And what are we making, little one?" Brave Wolf stood looking at his precious granddaughter. Although age had made simple things like walking and sleeping more difficult for him, the sight of this child brought joy to his heart and his aches and pains disappeared.

"It is a new basket for my treasures, my grandfather," said Smiling Fawn. "And why do you call me little one?" A frown crept across the girl's face as she spoke.

"You want to argue about that again?" asked Brave Wolf. "I thought we had an understanding . . ."

"Yes, yes, that is true," said Smiling Fawn. "But Mother Earth has danced with Brother Son twelve times since the day of my birth and I don't feel like a 'little one.'"

"May I sit while we talk, or would you have me stand until I fall?" Brave Wolf knew that a little joke would end their dispute.

"Oh, please . . . and sit here, Grandfather. The sun is not so bright." She put her weaving aside, rose, and helped him to the log bench.

"Ah, that is better," Brave Wolf said with a smile. "Now, I propose we talk of other things." From the corners of his eyes, he looked at Smiling Fawn and added, "If you think we should do so."

A wide grin spread across her face and she giggled, sounding very much like the little girl she no longer wanted to be. She sat opposite her grandfather so she could see his face. "Yes. We will talk of other things. And what would that be?"

Brave Wolf thought for a moment. "I believe I will tell a story about our valley, how it came to be. How this perfect green place was made for us."

With eyes sparkling and full of wonder, Smiling Fawn said in a very small voice, "I have never heard such a story, Grandfather."

"So now you will," whispered Brave Wolf, adding to the mystery of this new story.

With that, Smiling Fawn tucked her legs under herself and listened.

Ahote was resting after the long ordeal when he had helped the Great One complete all that is Mother Earth. In the space of three years' time, he had walked many miles. He had walked from ocean to ocean and from the highest mountains to the driest land. He had walked through endless snow and cold and across land so hot that it almost burned his feet. More times than he could count, he had watched Brother Sun and Sister Moon as they journeyed across the sky. All that time Ahote had done as he was instructed. Now he was tired.

Sleep would come easy as he stretched out beneath the low-hanging branches of a willow tree. The night was warm and the air was still. No bird or animal or

insect made a sound. He could hear nothing but the rhythmic sound of his own breathing. The sky was so clear Ahote imagined he could reach out and touch every one of the stars that floated above him. He smiled at the thought and stretched out one arm toward the heavens, grasping the air in the direction of one star and then another. He dropped his arm to his side and laughed at his own foolishness, for he knew it was impossible to touch a star. At length, Ahote heaved a great sigh, closed his eyes, and slept. And he dreamed.

In his dream, he found himself standing in the middle of a gently flowing stream, the water clear and warm. It was full daylight and Brother Sun hung overhead. He could see fish in the water all around him. On the riverbank, turtles of all sizes were sunning themselves on rocks and on the limbs of fallen trees. One or two slipped into the water and disappeared below its surface. A flock of ducks with brown, green, and blue feathers circled overhead and landed on the water. After some splashing and flapping and noisy greetings, one duck swam to the edge of the river and climbed onto the grassy shore. The others followed. As the ducks settled themselves, a single, large bird glided noiselessly above the middle of the stream, very close to the water, moving its wings just enough to stay in the air. Ahote ducked his head as it flew over him. He saw a flash of blue and gray, and the bird seemed to nod to him as it passed. He watched the large bird as it landed on a tree stump on the edge of the stream. Farther along, Ahote saw deer and foxes moving about in the

tall grass and among the trees. He saw squirrels, rabbits, beavers, and muskrats, some hurrying about, others content to sit or lie down. He heard the sounds of birds and saw them as they flitted among the trees and bushes. Out of the corner of his eye, he spied something orange, bright orange. He turned and saw bushes with deep green leaves and bright orange flowers swaying as the wind pushed them this way and that. Far away from the stream he could see hills— some rolling, some steep—that surrounded what he knew was a valley. It was such a beautiful place, such a peaceful place. If only . . .

Ahote awoke and sat up, the dream clear in his mind. He could still see the stream, the ducks, the birds, and animals, the bright orange flowers.

If only it were real, he thought. *If only it were real.* He lay down again with his hands behind his head, trying to remember all he had seen in his dream. And then one more thought: *I can make it so.*

Ahote crawled out from under the willow tree and stretched his arms over his head. He heard a soft "crack" in his right shoulder and wrapped his arms around his body to loosen the muscles. When he was satisfied, he set out in the early morning light to find the spring where he had rested a day ago. He needed to drink and to wash and to think about how he would "make it so."

With the first rays of Brother Sun at his back, Ahote arrived at the spring among the boulders. It bubbled

and danced to the surface from somewhere inside Mother Earth, making a small pool before the water ran down a gentle slope where it lost itself among reeds and bushes. The water was cold and tasted sweet. Ahote cupped his hands together and poured the water over his head and body. Yes, the water was cold! He shivered as it ran off his hair, down his arms, his stomach, his back, and his legs. After a few last gulps of the precious liquid, he wiped the water from his head, arms, and legs, and sat on a large rock that would soon be covered with Brother Sun's light and warmth.

In all his wanderings, Ahote had never seen anything like the place in his dream. He thought, *I will find such a place, and I will make it so.* Somewhere behind him, he heard a hawk call to its mate. Without understanding why, he turned and started walking in the direction of the sound.

At length, Ahote came to a field surrounded by gentle hills. There on the far side of the field he saw a family of foxes romping and running about in the warmth of the day. He watched for a little while, amused by the bundles of orange, brown, and white fur as they chased about among the grasses and small bushes in the meadow.

He called to them, and they stopped their play and watched as he approached them. At once, he recognized the dog and the vixen; they had crossed his path many times. Five healthy young kits were rolling in the soft grass, enjoying their first year.

"Hello, Renyard, I must ask you a question," said Ahote.

"Ah, friend Ahote. It is you," said the fox. When you called to us, my vixen and I were ready to run with our little ones to our cave. You have a question for me?"

"Indeed," Ahote replied. He described the place of his dream and asked, "Do you know of such a place, Renyard?"

The fox thought for a moment and shook his head. He looked at the vixen, but she shook her head as well. The fox said, "We have seen many streams and many valleys, but none are the valley you are seeking."

For a reason he could not explain, Ahote said, "Then come with me, and we will find it together."

The fox and the vixen agreed, and they, with their five kits, followed Ahote as he found his way up the nearest hill.

"But how did Ahote speak to the foxes, Grandfather?" asked Smiling Fawn. "Foxes make sounds like 'grrr' and 'rowf.' I do not understand."

"First," said Brave Wolf, "Ahote was wise beyond our understanding and able to speak to the animals. Perhaps he was able to put together all the 'grrrs' and 'rowfs' and other sounds so the foxes understood his meaning. Secondly, many unusual things happen in a legend. We must accept them as part of the story. As for the how of it, I cannot tell you. Now, shall I go on with the story?"

"Yes, please," said Smiling Fawn. "I want to hear it, all of it." As she had done since she was a child, Smiling Fawn

wrapped her arms around her drawn-up knees, rested her chin on them and waited.

Halfway up the hill, Ahote and the seven foxes saw a stag deer browsing among the low-hanging branches of an apple tree, looking for fruit and tender shoots. The stag was tall and lean; he proudly carried antlers with four points on each side. Every minute or so, the stag would raise his head to watch and listen for danger. Close by, his doe was feeding at another tree, while a small fawn had found a patch of clover and new grass.

Ahote had never seen this stag and doe before, so he spoke to them with great respect. "Ahem," he started, clearing his throat. "My friends and I have a question for you." Once again, Ahote described the place in his dream and asked if the deer had seen it.

The stag answered, "We have not. But it sounds like a good place."

The doe nodded her agreement as she chewed on a sweet, red apple and uttered a small grunt to the fawn who had wandered off a bit. Quickly, the young deer came to her mother's side.

"Will you help us find this place?" asked Ahote. "Surely we will find it."

The stag and the doe agreed, and the group had grown to eleven in number. With the young fawn at his side, Ahote led, and they made their way to the top of the hill and down to another field.

As he went on, Ahote found many animals and birds who joined him in his quest for the valley of his dream. There were field mice and squirrels, beavers and river otters, and even the skunk and his cousin, the mink. Great flocks of birds joined with Ahote: jays, the noisy wrens, and hawks of all kinds—birds of every size and shape. If it could be seen from above, it would have appeared to be a great migrating herd that stretched many miles as it moved across the land.

"Did all the animals and birds find the valley with Ahote?" asked Smiling Fawn.

"I understand," responded Brave Wolf. "You want to hear the end of the story. And it does have a fine ending. But it is best when all of a story is told, for there are many things to learn from such tales. Is that not true, little . . . my granddaughter?"

"Yes, that is true, Grandfather." And she laughed at his teasing. Then, as she had many times in her life, Smiling Fawn looked closely at the leathery, wrinkled face of her grandfather. He knew so much and wanted her to understand all he could tell of his people—her people—and their legends. So she listened . . .

One day as he led the great band of birds and animals toward the top of a hill, Ahote saw a large bird flying slowly toward him. He had seen it before but could not remember the time or the place. At length, the bird flew directly over his head, and he saw clearly the blue and gray feathers; it seemed to nod to him as it

flew past. The bird came to rest on a large rock at the crest of the hill. Carefully, it folded its long wings and stretched its long, thin neck and waited. It was nearly as tall as a child and sat motionless as Ahote came near.

He spoke to the blue-gray bird: "You are from my dream. You flew over my head while I stood in the stream . . . and nodded to me as you went by."

The bird made a soft grunting sound and slowly spread its wings and glided down the other side of the hill.

Quickly Ahote ran to the large rock. He wanted to watch the bird, to see where it might go. He saw so much more.

The bird flew high in the sky, its wings almost motionless as it glided along. It circled a few times and glided gracefully toward the valley floor. Ahote watched as the bird flew just above the water of a gently flowing stream that ran through the middle of a valley sparsely covered with coarse grass. The valley was without trees or bushes or flowers. It was, he thought, unfinished, waiting. And Ahote remembered his pledge: "I can make it so."

And that is what he did. Ahote, the Restless One, brought trees and bushes from other valleys to this, the valley of the river of his dream. He dug grasses from the hillsides and planted them in the valley. One day, while looking for more trees, he found a few bushes with dark green leaves and bright orange flowers. He pulled them from the ground and replanted them in the valley. In time, the new plants and trees and grasses

covered the valley as though the Great One had painted it. So beautiful was the valley that the great herd of animals and birds who followed Ahote to the valley remained there. In time, they were joined by more birds and more animals.

When it was finished, Ahote climbed to the top of the hill where he had first seen this place and looked down at the peaceful green valley. He smiled and thought to himself, *I have made it so.* He turned away and began walking, for it is told that the Restless One remained in one place for only a short time.

As Ahote stepped over a fallen oak tree, the shadow of a bird was clearly outlined on the ground in front of him. He looked toward the sky and shielded his eyes, for Brother Sun shone bright that day. Overhead he saw a large hawk covered with gray, brown, black, and white feathers that shimmered in the sun. Its head was covered with feathers of bright orange.

"Is that all, Grandfather?" Smiling Fawn asked. *"Only a hawk?"*

"Yes, my granddaughter, a hawk," he said. *"But perhaps not just any hawk."*

At once, she understood. Her face brightened and her eyes grew wide. "It was Shinaka, the hawk who came to guard the valley!"

Brave Wolf returned the smile and said, "Yes, the hawk is Shinaka." Then he asked, "What do you think about the story little . . . my not-so-little-granddaughter?"

Smiling Fawn nodded and replied, "It is a fine story, my grandfather. And I thank you for understanding I am not so little anymore."

SANCHEA

SANCHEA

"Grandfather," Smiling Fawn called brightly. "May I speak with you?"

"Just one moment," came the reply from behind the bearskin drawn across the doorway of the lodge.

It was a pleasant autumn day and Smiling Fawn wanted to spend some of it with her grandfather, Brave Wolf. She was in the thirteenth year of her life and thinking about becoming a full member of her tribe.

"Ah," said Brave Wolf as he came out of his lodge. "Brother Sun is playing tricks on us today. He shines his light but hides behind the clouds. Would you get my robe for me, the one with the drawing of the great bear on it? It will keep my shoulders warm."

The young girl found the robe hanging on the moose antlers above her grandfather's sleeping mat. She thought, I remember when he would wrap that robe around both of us as we sat by the fire on cold nights.

"Here, my grandfather, let me help you with it," said the girl as she walked to the old man.

"I will do it myself, little one," came the reply. He took the robe from her and draped it across his shoulders. "Now, what shall we speak of? Will it be animals or legends? Or do you have some news to tell me?"

They sat on the log bench in front of Brave Wolf's lodge.

When they were settled, the girl said in a serious voice, "Grandfather, when we see the face of Sister Moon three more times, I will celebrate Mezrat."

"Yes, that is true," said the old man. He waited, sensing that Smiling Fawn had more to say.

"I want to know about your mother, Sanchea," said the girl. "I want to hear her story." Smiling Fawn looked directly into her grandfather's eyes. "Will you tell it to me?"

"I can see this is important for you, my granddaughter," he said. "But tell me why."

Smiling Fawn tilted her head to one side and thought for a moment. "I think," she began. "No, I believe that to be a member of the Armaha, I must know the history of those who have gone before. And I want so much to know something of your mother, Sanchea."

Brave Wolf permitted himself a little smile and nodded his understanding. "All right. Here is the story as it was told to me by my mother."

With a strong voice, he began . . .

In the years before the Armaha moved into the green valley, they lived in high mountain valleys near the

mountain called Umaqua. The Kiowa and Comanche roamed the land to the northeast of Umaqua. The Chinook claimed lands far to the west by the great sea. The plains to the east of the great mountain were the home for the Arapaho and Dakota. To the south lay the great nation of the Otoe. The Armaha were content to live in the shadow of Umaqua, for she provided the water they needed for themselves, their horses, and their crops.

The Techlit were a tribe who occupied a vast territory north of Umaqua. They had come to this place from far beyond the peaceful sea that was told of in stories by hunters who had roamed far from the mountains toward the place where Brother Sun goes each day; they had roamed until they could roam no farther. The Techlit, it was told, had their origins in some far away land, a world where the mountains and valleys are white all year, and the air icy and forbidding. The stories told of how they had crossed a great sea of ice and found abundant food and trees for building their lodges. But the air was only a little warmer, and for almost half the year, they could not see Brother Sun. So the Techlit moved even farther south, first to lands covered with trees that remained green all year. That place was warmer, and the sea provided a bounty of food. But rains came often, sometimes for weeks on end.

In time, the Techlit found their way to the plains north of Umaqua, the mountain they called by the name Tolech, Proud Father. Here they were able to hunt for birds and animals of all kinds. The rivers and streams yielded fish and provided water for

their crops, for they had learned to grow grains and cultivate root vegetables. As the tribe prospered, it grew in number. From the first village there came a second and a third, then another and another until the Techlit claimed a vast territory as their own. And all the villages could see the great Tolech, for it was their belief that Tolech provided protection and assurance of long life.

Rehahn was an important leader in one of the villages. His wife was called Larka. Their first born was a boy, Reka, named for both his mother and his father. Rehahn was proud of the boy and proud that his firstborn was a son, for the Techlit believed this to be a good omen. A few years later, Sanchea was born, a lovely little girl with the darkest eyes ever seen in the tribe. Larka and Rehahn loved her and protected her. Even Reka made sure that his little sister was kept safe from harm.

"Grandfather," said Smiling Fawn quietly. "I have thought about brothers and sisters many times. About how it would be if White Sparrow and Strong Wolf had brought other children into the world. How it would be if I had a brother."

Brave Wolf spoke carefully: "You know, my grand-daughter, your parents had almost lost hope of having children of their own when you came into the world. But you are enough to give them joy." Then in a different voice, "And you have many friends in the tribe, almost like brothers and sisters. Is that not so?"

"Yes, Grandfather," she replied. "But still I wonder."

She smoothed the edge of her deerskin skirt. Brave Wolf knew it was her way of thinking serious thoughts.

At length, she folded her hands in her lap and said quietly, "I cannot change what is, can I? I must be content with all the Great One has given to me and my people." In a stronger voice she said, "Please tell me more of Sanchea's story."

Brave Wolf reached for her hand and held it for a moment before continuing . . .

Sanchea grew into a fine girl, not beautiful by any means, but pure of heart, honest, and caring. By the time she had reached her eleventh year, the younger children would gather around her and beg for Sanchea to tell a story. Sometimes she repeated a favorite story the children wanted to hear again. Other times, she would create a new story for them, putting it together as she spoke, not really sure where it might lead. The children were attentive, giggling and "oohing" in all the right places, even clapping their hands when something humorous or unexpected happened in the story. And when they gave their approval, Sanchea would smile, her face lighting up the circle or the room. And it was her smile that made Sanchea different from other girls her age. For it radiated a beauty that came from within, something one cannot hide from others.

Two years hence, Sanchea was preparing for Frech-Comta, passage to the world, a ceremony each member of the tribe was led through in their thirteenth year. It signaled the time when the world of childhood gives way to the responsibilities of adulthood.

The ceremony was simple enough. On the appointed day—that day determined by the Council of Elders—the boy or girl was led with eyes covered to the sacred place where offerings and praise were given to the Great One. Here were gathered all the adults of the tribe, arranged by age in three circles of benches, one inside the other— the eldest in the inner circle, the youngest in the outer circle. As the blindfolded girl or boy was led to the center of the circle, the tribal chief began a special song. After one line of the song, he was joined by the other elders. All other adults joined the chorus when the third line was sung. On this day, they sang for Sanchea.

We gaze upon the Great Tolech who guards and protects us.

Our hearts are filled with love for him.

O, Great One, hear us as we bring Sanchea to you

For your blessing and for your favor.

The Great One speaks straight to our hearts

And makes us smile with joy.

With Tolech always in our sight, forever protecting us,

We give our lives to you.

We ask that you accept our gift of life

In the person of Sanchea.

As she sheds the cloak of childhood and childish ways,

Allow her to take her rightful place.

As the final strains of the song echoed and faded away, Rehahn and Larka arose, walked to their daughter's side, removed the scarlet cloth that covered her eyes, and placed it around her shoulders. After warm embraces, dampened only a little by the tears in Larka's eyes, all the other adults arose as one and sang the song once more. And as they sang, Larka, Rehahn, and Sanchea walked among them so all could touch her and welcome her to this new station in life. When Sanchea stood before her brother, Reka picked her up and whirled her around, bringing sounds of laughter and clapping hands from the gathering. And this brought a smile and unrestrained laughter from Sanchea. The women of the tribe nodded to one another: In two or three years, Sanchea would be a good match for some lucky young man.

While the ceremony was taking place, the younger children remained in the village, fetching wood for the council fire. Carefully, they stacked the logs, filling the voids with small pieces of kindling and dry grasses. All was supervised by Pehcek, a young man of fifteen. The children did their work eagerly, for that was the way of the Techlit. A task was to be carried out with pleasure and done to the best of one's ability. That is not to say that the work was done without a few antics here and there.

When the pile of wood was complete, Pehcek made one last inspection to make sure it had been done properly. He was surprised to see a large sunflower that appeared to grow from the very top of the waiting pile. The culprits were soon identified, two boys who often played tricks on others. They were instructed to climb to the top of the pile and remove the offending flower. With a little encouragement, they made their way over and among the logs and did as they were told. As they handed the sunflower to Pehcek, he said, "Now, little friends, take the sunflower back to the top of the pile. Perhaps we can feed a few birds before the fire is set."

The boys hesitated, unsure if they should do as Pehcek instructed, thinking it might just be a joke. But Pehcek swatted each on his behind and said, "Go, and do it quickly before the others return."

The boys seemed to swim up the pile, each one standing at the top, giving the pose of a conqueror. This, of course, was done to the joy and delight of the other children. Two young girls about the same age

as the two offenders whispered and giggled to one another, both with thoughts of what might be in a few years. Once back down on the ground, Pehcek gave the boys a gentle slap on the back as if to say, "Well done."

And it was none too soon, for the adults were walking noisily into the center of the village. Rehahn and Larka led the procession, with Sanchea and Reka close behind. When the younger children saw their beloved Sanchea, they ran to her as if a swarm of bees or hummingbirds to their favorite flower. Instinctively, Sanchea reached down and picked up the smallest boy; he was in the fourth year of his life, and although she had never said so, he was one of her favorites. The children squealed with excitement asking Sanchea about the ceremony. And they asked if she would tell them a story.

Sanchea considered their request for a moment and asked them to listen to her carefully. "I want very much to tell you a story, perhaps the one about the fox and the beaver; I know it is one you like. But you must understand that Sanchea now has other responsibilities in the tribe. And so we will select a time on one day each week when we can gather together, a time for me to tell stories. Who knows? Perhaps one of the other girls or boys will tell you stories."

Her words were met with silence, and she continued, speaking again to the children. "Tonight, when the fire is lit, you and I will sing the song we learned not long ago, the one about great Tolech and the mountain goat. I think it will be great fun, and your parents will be proud to hear your voices. Can we do that?"

"Yes," they all shouted, "Yes, we can."

And with that, the children ran to be with their parents. All, that is, but the little boy in Sanchea's arms. It had been a long day, and he had fallen asleep, with his head nestled comfortably on her shoulder. She took him to his mother, who gently lifted the child from the young woman. They exchanged smiles and the mother nodded her thanks to Sanchea.

Sanchea went to her mother and asked if she would walk with her for a while. Larka took her daughter's arm, and they found the path that led to the broad stream where they could sit on a flat boulder and enjoy the last warmth of the sun. Along the way, they spoke of common things: how fine the weather was for the ceremony, surely a good sign for the future; how Reka had surprised his sister by picking her up and swinging her around; how well the children had built the fire for tonight.

Finally at the stream, Larka and Sanchea found a likely rock and sat. The lengthening shadows and slanting rays of the afternoon sun made the stream shimmer and sparkle. A light breeze set trees and bushes to swaying. They had found a peaceful place. Larka smoothed her dress and waited for her daughter to speak.

Sanchea said, "I disliked very much having to speak to the children as I did. I thought I was doing what is expected of me, but something inside hurt when I spoke."

Larka responded with care. "When we reach our thirteenth year, we become responsible members of the tribe and must step away from things we did before—"

"But, my mother," interrupted Sanchea.

"No," said Larka, a mild rebuke. "You must listen to what I have to say." She patted her daughter's hand and held it. "You told the children that there must be a change, but you also told them that they will be able to hear your stories. That is good. And there might be another way."

"Another way?" Sanchea asked. She waited for her mother's response.

"You love the children, my daughter, and they love you," said Larka quietly. "They come to you because they trust you. Even though they are young, they know you will treat them with dignity. It is a rare trait for such a young person."

Sanchea smiled. "Yes, I love them. It is as if they are my own. And I care about them—worry about them. Is that wrong, my mother?"

Now Larka laughed. "No, no. To care and to love is good. But we must find a way for you to use that love and care." Larka changed her tone ever so slightly. "Do you remember the old man, the Kiowa who wandered into our village?"

"Yes," said Sanchea. "He was lost, tired, almost at the end of his life."

"And do you remember how you were able to learn his language? It was easy for you, my daughter."

Sanchea's cheeks reddened. She was embarrassed in her own self-pride.

Larka continued. "And the Dakota warrior. Your father found him watching our village and brought him here. You learned some of his language, too."

Sanchea spoke softly, with respect. "Perhaps the Great One lets me hear and understand others who speak a different language."

"Yes, my daughter. And you can teach the children to understand others. You will teach them what you know of the Kiowa and Dakota tongues. It is a start. I think it is good."

Sanchea smiled. "And I will be able to spend some time with the children."

Larka arose and straightened her dress, a sign that they should return to the village. With just a trace of a smile—for she didn't want to pour too much pride on her daughter—she said, "Come. Our chief and his woman will want to spend a few moments with you. And we must prepare for tonight."

The two women retraced their steps to the village in silence, both considering what they had said and heard there by the stream, at the same time knowing that their relationship had changed. They walked

arm-in-arm, two friends with deep love and respect, understanding the strength and wisdom each brings to the world.

"My granddaughter," said Brave Wolf as he rose to his feet. "Let us go into my lodge. The air is cool, and I would like to sit by my fire for a while."

"Oh, I am sorry, Grandfather," said the girl. "I did not know . . ."

"It is all right, little one," said the old man. "I think we both found ourselves inside the story. And when that happens, we think of nothing else. Here, let me hold the bearskin aside."

They entered the lodge and found the mats they had sat on many times before. The mat Brave Wolf chose had the image of Umaqua on it. Smiling Fawn's mat, her favorite, was woven with the image of the great hawk, Shinaka. Smiling Fawn added a few branches and other pieces of wood to the fire in the center of the lodge and worked with

them until the fire glowed with a comforting warmth.

Brave Wolf said, "Yes, that is better. Sometimes my shoulders . . . But that is not important. We have a story to finish."

Smiling Fawn looked at her grandfather with worry in her eyes and asked, "Your shoulders, Grandfather?"

"It is nothing, little one," he said. "Let me go on . . ."

As the last rays of Brother Sun disappeared from the sky, torches were set to the pile of logs. The small sticks and dry grass glowed brightly, and soft smoke rose in the air. Soon the logs were in flames, turning night into day. The children giggled and squealed and talked in hushed tones as the flames mounted toward the night sky. At a signal from Sanchea, they stood and gathered near her and sang the song that told the story of Tolech and the baby mountain goat. As they sang, they swayed and moved their feet to the rhythm of the song, a little dance that Sanchea had taught them. And when the song was done, they jumped and hopped around the roaring fire as the tribe clapped their hands in approval.

When the children had returned to sit with their families, two women began a song. It told the legend of their ancestors, how a handsome tribesman and a young maiden had met and fallen in love, how all the Techlit descended from these two. As others joined in the song, the young man Benak approached Sanchea and nodded toward the fire. He was asking her to dance with him. She rose and followed him to an open space where they stood apart from each other and began to sway. After a few moments, he held out his hand, and she took it, a sign that she accepted his show of interest. They did not dare look at each other, for that would displease Tolech and the Great One. These things needed to be done in the proper way. When the song ended, Sanchea and Benak walked in different directions and returned to their families. Larka had watched their dance with great interest; she permitted her lips to show just the hint of a smile when her daughter sat down next to her. Larka remembered once more how she had danced with Rehahn not seventeen years ago. And so, it was with her daughter, for the Great One had made it so.

In the following days, Sanchea and Larka visited the homes of the elders. It was expected after the celebration of Frech-Comta for the young girl or boy to pay respects to the leaders and their women. Each meeting was the same. At the time agreed to, Larka stood in front of the dwelling and said, "Sanchea brings you greetings." With that, the elder's wife came to the door and invited Larka and Sanchea to enter. Sanchea then went directly to the elder who was seated facing the door, for that was the place of honor. Sanchea bowed slightly and asked if she might sit and speak with him. The elder motioned to the girl to sit on his left side. Once Sanchea was seated, the elder's wife sat on his right side and Larka next to her. It was a ritual that the Techlit had brought with them from that other land of cold and ice and snow. The visit consumed only a little time, but it satisfied the elder that the young boy or girl had been raised properly according to beliefs of the Techlit.

There were nine elders in the village, and Sanchea and Larka repeated this ritual on nine consecutive days immediately after the morning meal. When all the visits had been made, the elders met and decided what role Sanchea would have in the tribe.

A few days after her last visit with the elders, Sanchea rose early. She started the fire for the morning meal and walked to the stream to bring fresh water. The day was clear and cool, the rising sun coloring the clouds with shades of orange and pink. She swung the wooden pail as she walked and sang a song her mother used to sing to her when she was very young. It told of how Sister Moon protects us while we sleep.

I am the silver light that guides your dreams.

I am the one who watches while you sleep,

Rest well, my little ones for you are tired

And wake to greet the day when I am gone.

The scarlet cloth wrapped around her shoulders felt good on such a cool morning. She wore it often. It was the cloth that had covered her eyes during Frech-Comta; Sanchea thought of it as a treasure to be

honored and protected. When not being worn, it was folded neatly and placed at the end of her straw sleeping mat.

As she came to the stream, Sanchea sensed that she was not alone, that some animal or some person was nearby, watching. She put down the wooden pail and listened. There it was, a sound behind her. She turned and saw Benak standing in the path with hands on his hips. Sanchea looked at him and said nothing.

Benak spoke. "So, you are up early making a fire and fetching water. And what else?"

"Nothing else," Sanchea responded flatly. Her face showed no emotion as she watched the boy before her. Among the Techlit, young boys and girls should not be together unless with their parents or other adults. For what young man would want such a maiden to be his wife?

Benak broke the silence. Walking toward Sanchea, he said, "You took my hand, and we danced together. The tribe knows you have accepted my show of interest. I do not know of any other who has approached you."

"You do not know everything, Benak." A small shiver ran up Sanchea's spine. "Perhaps you should return to the village."

Suddenly, the boy was directly in front of her. He spoke. "Perhaps I will. And perhaps it will be after you favor me with a kiss."

He reached out with both arms to hold the girl by her shoulders. Sanchea backed away and dropped

her head. Her heart was pounding, and she was afraid. Dancing in front of the tribe was one thing. But kissing was something far beyond that, and she would not give that favor to Benak. Sanchea was sorry she had accepted his hand, sorry she had danced with him. Once more, Benak moved toward her, this time taking hold of her left arm. The girl tried to pull away, but Benak's hold was firm. As he bent his head to kiss her, Sanchea swung with her right arm and slapped his face.

The boy became enraged; he would never let some girl humiliate him like that, even a maiden as desirable as this one. Benak held a hand to his burning left cheek and spoke in a growl. "I will have my kiss, Sanchea, and I will have it now!"

He lunged at the girl and grabbed both of her arms, pinning them to her sides. Instinctively, Sanchea stomped on his right foot. Benak released his grip and cried out in pain. Sanchea saw her chance. She pushed Benak out of the way and started running toward the path. The wooden pail and the water were long forgotten. She needed to be in her own home where her parents and her brother would protect her. And so she ran.

As Sanchea reached the path, she stumbled, tripped by a rock, and fell to the ground. Benak had forgotten his sore foot and was nearly upon her. She got to her feet and started running once again, now terrified and crying. She took one quick glance over her shoulder at the sneering face of Benak. He yelled at her, calling her "Zarchow," an unclean woman.

As Sanchea whipped her head toward the path, something struck her left eye. After a few steps, the pain came, searing, like no pain she had ever experienced before. She fell to her knees and cried out to Benak to help her. But she was alone. And she could see nothing out of her left eye.

Sanchea cried out once more. "Benak, help me . . . my eye." And then the scene before her seemed to swim, and the world went black.

"Grandfather," cried Smiling Fawn. "You are telling me bad things again. You know that makes me sad."

"There is sadness in this story, my granddaughter," he said. "And remember, this is not a legend. These things happened. It is only the truth."

"But a stick in the eye!" said the girl. "How terrible for Sanchea. How terrible for your mother."

"Yes. Terrible at the time," he replied. "But before the story ends you will come to know her strength. You will come to know much about my mother, Sanchea."

"I . . . I think I understand, Grandfather," said the young girl. "Please go on."

"Sanchea! Sanchea!" It was Reka's voice. Her brother was sitting on the ground holding her close to him. "Rehahn could not find you and sent me. What has happened?"

"I came to the stream for water . . ." Sanchea was about to tell all of what happened but stopped, afraid that she would have to reveal that she had been alone with Benak. The punishment would be severe. "I . . . I fell against the bushes, and something struck my eye."

"I can see that," said Reka. "A nasty wound."

Reka helped Sanchea to her feet and steadied her as they walked back to the village.

"The water," said Sanchea, pointing towards the stream.

"Not now. I will see to it after we get you back to our lodge." Reka held onto his sister.

Once Sanchea was safely in her own lodge, Larka cleaned the wound and covered the damaged left eye. In the days that followed, Larka changed the dressing several times each day, each time looking for some sign of healing. Nothing Larka could do seemed to help. Even the older women who knew much about sickness, wounds, and healing were baffled by Sanchea's injury. In the end, the girl's left eye was milky, sightless.

Even before the chief summoned them, Rehahn and Larka knew they would have to give up their daughter. An injury to the body—a broken arm or a wound to the stomach or leg—was acceptable. But the loss of an eye was a bad omen, an act of the Great One or Tolech, the Proud Father. Perhaps even

both had caused it to happen. No matter. Sanchea must leave her people, must leave the Techlit to appease the Great One and the Proud Father.

On the fifteenth day after she had celebrated Frech-Comta, her passage to the world became total exile from the people and the life she loved. Once again blindfolded with the scarlet cloth, her father took her far from Tolech and left Sanchea sitting against a tree beside the trail. Her eyes were still covered and her hands bound behind her. No words were exchanged between them during the three-day journey. The elders had demanded, and Rehahn had obeyed. When he returned to the village, he and Larka would observe a period of mourning. Sanchea was dead, her name never again to be said aloud.

Sanchea submitted to the punishment because she believed it to be fair. The Techlit had lived with these beliefs since time began, and a young girl such as she could not change that. And she kept her silence about Benak. She was certain that events of the future would repay him for what he had done.

When Rehahn bound Sanchea's hands, he made sure the rope would loosen. For most of one day, Sanchea sat by the tree twisting her wrists this way and that inside the rope. As Brother Sun fell from the sky, she was able to slip her hands free. At that instant, a wave of shame and sadness came over her, and she sobbed, recounting all that had happened to her in her short life. She held her head in her hands and said aloud to herself, "O, Great One. O, Proud Father. I know the stain that is my left eye displeases you. But I am young; I am strong. I can serve you. If I cannot serve the Techlit, my people, help me find others to serve. I ask these things with humility."

"I am sad again, Grandfather," said Smiling Fawn. "Left alone by her own father."

"It was the way of the Techlit, little one," said Brave Wolf. "Rehahn did only what he knew to be right. He had no choice."

"But when will I hear of happy things in your story?" she asked.

"Well," he replied. "If you let me go on, I think you will hear some happy things, even joyous things. And remember," he said, looking directly in her eyes, "this is not just my story. It is our story."

"Yes, Grandfather," she said, smiling. "Please go on with our story."

"Are you lost, little one?" It was Gray Wolf, a young man and member of the Armaha tribe. He was part of a hunting party that had ranged far to the northern edge of their lands.

"Yes ... no ... I ..." Was all Sanchea could say. But their languages were very different, and they could not understand each other.

Finally, Gray Wolf pointed at his chest and slowly said, "Gray Wolf."

Sanchea tried to repeat what she had heard, but it sounded like, "Grry Off."

He tried again, this time even slower. After several more attempts, he was ready to give up.

"Grayee Wooolf?" asked Sanchea.

He nodded, showing she was correct, then pointed to her.

"San-che-ya," she said slowly, hoping he would understand.

After a half hour of trying and failing, Gray Wolf and Sanchea knew each other's names and the names of their tribes. Gray Wolf understood only that something had happened, and the girl had been left here. He led her to the small clearing where the rest of the hunting party was settling for the night.

A few days later, the hunters returned to the village of the Armaha with much game to feed the tribe and with this strange young girl with the milky eye. The people of the village could see that Sanchea had endured something terrible. A few of the Armaha women approached her. Then seeing her sightless, milky left eye, they backed away, unsure, afraid.

Finally, the woman whom they called Old Mother came to Sanchea and led her to a small dwelling set apart from the other lodges. Without a word, the woman offered her sleeping mat to Sanchea and the young girl sat down. The woman brought a bowl of warm broth that smelled of wild mushrooms and spices. Sanchea drank it eagerly, her first real nourishment in four days. The woman bathed Sanchea's face, neck, and arms with water scented with wild flowers and pine bark. As she tended to the young girl, Old Mother hummed a strange tune. Sanchea stretched out on the sleeping mat and laid her head on a small leather pouch filled with straw. And she slept.

Sanchea heard the woman humming and opened her eyes. She rolled her head to the left to get a clear picture. Old Mother was sitting on a small mat stitching a leather pouch much like the one Sanchea rested on. The woman spoke, but Sanchea did not understand the language. Sanchea sat up and started to explain how she came to be in this place, but the woman waved a hand and shook her head.

Sanchea asked a simple question. "Kiowa?"

The woman's eyes brightened, and in that language, she answered with surprise, "You speak Kiowa!"

From that moment, Sanchea and Old Mother were nearly inseparable. The woman helped Sanchea regain her strength and her confidence. She took the young girl to the spring where water was drawn each day. There Sanchea met the other women of the village. Old Mother taught Sanchea the ways of the Armaha, the important rituals and taboos. And she taught Sanchea their language. In time, Sanchea told the woman about Benak and how she injured her eye. Sanchea would live with Old Mother for almost two years.

It was a sad day for Sanchea when Old Mother went to live with the Great One. Her closest friend was gone, and Sanchea felt abandoned. The other women of the village had accepted Sanchea as one of their own, but she was unable to find a friend like Old Mother. Most of the time Sanchea found herself alone.

One day in her fifteenth year, she was carrying a bundle of clothes she had washed in the stream. As Sanchea stepped into a clearing she heard a voice.

"May I speak with you, Sanchea?" It was Gray Wolf, the young man who had found her along the trail.

Sanchea almost dropped the bundle. "Yes you may speak with me. But why startle me like this?" She was trying to sound annoyed.

Gray Wolf went on. "I am sorry if I scared you, Sanchea. I only . . ."

She cut him off. "You did not scare me. You startled me. Perhaps you know there is a difference." Sanchea waited, the bundle growing heavier every second.

"Yes. I am sorry if I startled you. If we walk back to your lodge, you can put those wet clothes down and give your arms a rest." Gray Wolf waited with arms crossed.

Without a word, Sanchea walked around Gray Wolf and through the clearing and returned to her small lodge.

The next day Sanchea was busy in her lodge when she heard Gray Wolf's voice. "May I speak with you, Sanchea?" She thought, *Is this the only question he knows?*

She stepped outside. The sun shining behind Gray Wolf made his image shimmer. Sanchea shaded her eyes. She could see clearly the patch of gray in his otherwise jet black hair.

Without emotion she said, "You want to speak with me?"

Gray Wolf responded. "In another year, you will be expected to choose a young man to be your husband. Because I am older than you by two years, our custom allows me to tell you I would be pleased if you chose me. That is what I wanted to say to you."

"And if I choose another or no one . . . ?"

"Then," said Gray Wolf, a note of disappointment in his voice, "it will be a sad thing for Gray Wolf." And he walked away, striding with the confidence his father had taught.

Sanchea walked back into her home, the small lodge she had shared with Old Mother. The tasks she had planned for the day were forgotten. Gray Wolf's words filled her mind. ". . . you will be expected to choose a young man . . ." This is something Old Mother had not told her.

Her sixteenth year was coming to an end, and Sanchea had not yet made the selection that was

expected of her. In the Techlit tribe, things were much different. Young men came to a girl's mother and father and asked to speak to her and her parents. When a few or several young men had made such a visit, the girl and her mother would decide which young men would be considered, and they would be encouraged to call again. This continued until one young man would be asked to come speak with the girl and her parents. At that meeting, he would ask for the girl, and she and her parents would agree.

But here among the Armaha, she would have to make the choice on her own without the advice of her mother.

Soon Sister Moon would show her full face and Sanchea would reach her seventeenth year. But she was no closer to making the choice required of her than she was when Gray Wolf had first told her of his interest—and he had been the only one.

A few days later, Sanchea came out of her lodge with a leather pouch she had stitched for one of the women in the village. As she was about to announce herself at the woman's lodge, she chanced to look to her right and saw Gray Wolf speaking with a very young girl. He was on his knees holding her shoulders. Her knees were dirty and skinned, and the girl had been crying. Sanchea heard the girl thank Gray Wolf and tell him she felt better and would be careful. The young girl wiped her eyes and skipped toward her own lodge. Sanchea walked to Gray Wolf.

"And what happened to that little girl?" she asked.

"Oh, Sanchea," Gray Wolf said as he rose. "She and some others were running, and she tripped on a tree root. She landed on her knees. She was not hurt badly. But little ones think any bruise or scrape is serious. She was crying, so I picked her up and stayed with her until she felt better."

"That was a kind thing to do," said Sanchea. "Not every young man would have done so." After saying it, she realized she had praised Gray Wolf, and she felt the warmth on her cheeks.

"Perhaps not," he replied. "But if we are not careful with our young ones, what is to become of the Armaha?"

"Sanchea. Sanchea." It was the woman for whom she had made the leather pouch. The voice came from only a few paces away but sounded as if coming from a great distance.

After a moment, Sanchea realized who had called her name. She smiled shyly at Gray Wolf, turned, and walked to the woman at the door of her lodge.

On the last day of her sixteenth year, Sanchea told Gray Wolf she was choosing him to be her husband. He accepted her announcement with folded arms, permitting the corners of his mouth to rise just a little, for a broad grin or smile would not suit a man such as he.

Three months later, in accordance with Armaha custom, they were bound as husband and wife by the senior elder of the tribe. Following the brief ceremony where Sanchea and Gray Wolf made a pledge, one to the other, the women of the village provided a feast of meats, fishes, breads, and cakes. At one end of the village, the Armaha danced and sang long into the night, while the young man and woman spent their first night together in Sanchea's small lodge.

As he studied his granddaughter, Brave Wolf said, "In time, Sanchea would bring two sons into the world. But that is a story you have heard and know."

"Yes, my grandfather," said Smiling Fawn. "Your brother Gray Deer and you. I remember well that part of the story. I mean that part of our story."

With that, Smiling Fawn threw her arms around her grandfather and held him for a moment. He put his hands on her head and smiled to himself, and thought, Surely the Armaha would be proud to have such a fine young woman as a member of the tribe.

AMA

What shall I wish for this year, my grandfather?"
Smiling Fawn asked with a very serious look on
her young face. "When the snow stops falling
and Brother Sun shines so bright on Umaqua, I always
make a wish. But I can think of nothing to wish for," she
said. "I need your help."

Brave Wolf was sitting in his lodge when his granddaughter came to the door and said these things. He had
been repainting his favorite long pipe with a feather and red
dye made from clay and the juice of berries from the sour
gum tree that shaded the entrance to the lodge. Carefully, he
set the pipe, the small pot of dye, and the feather aside and
looked up at the girl. In the fourteenth year of her life,
Smiling Fawn was poised on the fine, sometimes bewilder-
ing edge between girl and young woman. Just last year, she
had celebrated Mezrat, the Passage, and she understood
clearly and fully what was expected of a young woman. But
on one occasion or another she would come to her grandfather seeming to be the little girl of her past. Brave Wolf could
see this was one of those times. He permitted the edges of his
mouth to turn up into the trace of a smile and motioned for
Smiling Fawn to enter the lodge and sit.

The east-facing lodge had but one room. It was a rather small, rectangular structure and made of logs. The roof was constructed of thin saplings covered with pine branches. Light entered from the doorway and from a single hole in the roof that also served as a chimney for the round, stone fireplace. The dirt floor was covered with pine boughs and woven mats and rugs that carried the important symbols of the Armaha: the bear, the wolf, the hawk, Brother Sun, Sister Moon, and the mountain Umaqua, the Sacred House. In the cold months, when Umaqua was covered with snow, a large bearskin hung across the door. But now, the snow was gone, and the air felt warm; the bearskin had been set out of the way and hung on the wall next to the door. The shining face of Brother Sun lighted the room almost completely.

Smiling Fawn looked for her favorite mat, the one showing the great hawk, and saw it was directly across from her grandfather. As she settled on it, Brave Wolf spoke in even tones. "I am pleased to see you, little one."

She didn't like to be called "little one" and started to protest, but before she could speak, he placed his left hand on her arm and went on.

"I am pleased, little one," he said with emphasis on the two words. "And I wonder: Why would a young member of the tribe speak at length to an elder without first asking for permission?" He waited.

In a quiet voice, Smiling Fawn replied, "I . . . I am sorry, Grandfather. I . . . I forgot."

"That is correct, Smiling Fawn. You forgot. And what are the promises one makes . . . the promises you made at Mezrat? Do you remember?"

Smiling Fawn tilted her head to one side. In her mind, she recalled clearly the ceremony called Mezrat when she became a full member of the tribe. Sister Moon had shown her face only four times since that wonderful day. She thought for a moment and then, remembering the words she recited at Mezrat, she replied, this time with confidence, "I promise to give my life to Mother Earth. I promise to hold the honor of the Armaha in my heart. I promise to use my mind and my strength for good. I promise to respect my elders and to treat them with deference. I promise to live with a happy heart all my days."

"Yes," said Brave Wolf. "You do remember." He waited for a moment, looking at his granddaughter. At length, he wiped away a single tear that had found its way from her right eye onto her cheek. The old man smiled and with a twinkle in his eye, he asked in a very serious voice, "Now, what is this great problem I can help you solve?"

The young woman smiled, understanding that her scolding was over. She smoothed the front of her dress and tilted her head a little to one side. It was a habit she carried from her earliest days. Then she spoke softly. "Ever since I was a little girl, I have made a wish each spring. I can think of nothing to wish for this spring, and I come to you for help."

"All right," Brave Wolf replied. "Perhaps a story will help you find your wish."

A legend is told of a young maiden who lived long before the Armaha came to this green valley. In the legend, her name is Ama. Like so many of the people

we hear of in legend, Ama lived alone. We don't know where she lived, but the legend tells that she lived near mountains in a dry, arid place where very few plants and trees grew.

Ama was a beautiful young woman—tall, slender. She moved in an effortless manner, seeming to glide across the ground when she walked. Her black hair was long, hanging beyond her waist, and was often adorned with wild flowers or vines. Her dark eyes were clear and gentle, almost sad. Ama's voice could be soft and sweet. But if she saw injustice, she spoke with a firm, sure voice.

One day as Ama was walking on a trail toward the mountain, she met a small deer limping along the same trail but going in the opposite direction. Ama was wise in the ways of many animals and spoke to the deer. "Are you hurt, my little friend?"

This deer had never spoken to a human before, so it stopped and backed away with its tail held low. Its large, brown eyes were wide, and its muzzle quivered with fear. The deer pawed nervously at the ground.

In a soft, soothing voice, Ama said, "Do not be afraid, my friend, Ama will do you no harm. Now, why are you limping? A stone in your hoof perhaps?"

The deer answered, "No, not a stone in my hoof. I think a thorn or briar." Carefully and slowly, he raised his left rear hoof so Ama could look at it and continued speaking. "And I have had no water to drink all day."

She held the hoof gently in one hand and stroked the deer's neck with the other. The animal stood quietly, yielding to Ama's soft voice and hands. Ama saw the thorn from a cactus that had found its way into the soft flesh between the toes of the hoof.

"Be brave, my friend," said Ama. "Your discomfort will soon be gone." Once more, she stroked the deer's neck and quickly removed the thorn. The deer made a small painful sound and then became quiet as Ama rubbed the sore flesh. Carefully, the deer set the hoof down and put his weight on it.

"It feels much better now. How can I thank you?" asked the deer.

Ama replied, "Someday you will have a chance to help another animal or a human. That will repay me quite well. As for water, I wish I could do more, but I cannot help you."

With that, Ama stroked the deer's back, scratched it behind the ears, and bid it good-bye.

"Grandfather," interrupted Smiling Fawn, unable to remain silent. "There is something about this story. What is it?"

"Something about the story?" asked the old man. "I don't quite know what you mean," he said in a surprised voice. "Shall I go on?"

"Yes," said the young woman. "But there is still something . . ."

Brave Wolf went on before she could finish her thought . . .

Closer to the mountain, the trail began to rise from the dry land, and as the trail became steep, Ama could feel the pull on her legs. The dusty trail twisted and turned among the rocks like a huge snake. Ama rounded a bend in the trail and saw a small lizard sitting in the shade of a large boulder. Its leathery green skin looked rough and hard. Slowly, the lizard looked this way and that, while blinking its eyes sleepily. His long forked tongue flicked at the air.

"Hello, my lizard friend," said Ama quietly. "You should be sitting on that boulder to warm yourself."

The lizard jumped at the sound of her voice, but he was afraid of no one. He turned to Ama, stared at her as fiercely as he could, and said in a loud voice, "I have had all the sun I need today, thank you." And with that, he flicked his long, forked tongue at an unsuspecting bug, which disappeared in the lizard's mouth. "Besides that, something is sticking in my back, and it makes me angry."

In a very serious voice, Ama said, "Yes, that would make anyone angry." Then she asked, "May I look at your back to see what is sticking there?"

"Of course," answered the lizard as he waddled toward Ama.

She saw the thorn, just at the base of the lizard's tail. She held it between her thumb and finger and pulled it out. "There," she said.

"Ouch!" said the lizard, turning toward her once again. "You should tell someone before you do that," he said angrily.

Ama laughed. "Better?" she asked.

"Yes, yes," the lizard replied. "But a few sips of water are what I need. Yes, water, that's what I need."

Ama wished she could do more, but explained she could not help him. She bid the lizard a good day and continued on the trail up the side of the mountain.

As she trudged along, Ama thought about her encounters with the deer and the lizard. Both were weary from the heat, both had been injured by the thorn of a cactus, and both were thirsty. Beyond sympathy and removing thorns, there was little she could do for them. But how could she or anyone or any animal help them find water?

"But, Grandfather," said Smiling Fawn with great excitement. "Her name is Ama . . ."

"Yes, Granddaughter," he said. "Now let me finish the story."

Ama continued up the slope and found her way to a high, bowl-shaped valley near the top of the great mountain. The cooler air and a light breeze combined to make it a most pleasant place. Feeling tired now, she stretched out next to a pile of rocks. Soon her mind and body gave in, and she fell into a deep sleep.

During her sleep, she heard the voice of the Great One in a dream: "You have pleased me, Ama. Your quick mind, gentle ways, and kind heart give me

great pride, for that is how I created you. But there is more you can do for the animals of my world. And for Mother Earth herself. Listen to me . . ."

When she awoke, Sister Moon had taken Brother Sun's place in the sky. Ama remembered all the Great One had spoken in her dream. Obediently, she walked to the floor of the valley, clearly visible by the silver light shining above her. She found the bed of flowers the Great One had told her about, removed her simple gown, and lay on the flowers clad only in her tunic as she had been instructed in her dream.

The light of Sister Moon was almost warm on her skin as she lay on the soft flowers. In a short time, she felt herself somehow rise from the valley floor. She could look down and see that her body was still lying on the bed of flowers. And as she watched, her body became a pool of water that spread and rose. The water lapped at the stones and small plants near the bed of flowers. Soon all was covered: the flowers, her body, nearby stones, rocks, and boulders. Before Sister Moon had completed her journey across the sky, the valley had become a vast lake filled with water. A few minutes before Brother Sun appeared, the waters of the lake found their way to the edge of the trail that Ama had walked. Then the water tumbled over the edge and poured down the mountain to the valley below.

The earth-bound Ama had ceased to be. And yet, as she watched all of it unfold, here in the realm of the

Great One, she smiled, knowing she had found water for the animals—and for Mother Earth as well. She had surely found her destiny. And she hoped all the birds and animals and peoples of the world would find theirs.

Smiling Fawn could contain her excitement no longer. "The name, Ama. It means water! She gave herself so we could have water."

"That is right," said Brave Wolf. "Can you make your wish now, little . . . I mean, my granddaughter?"

"Yes, I can make my wish. And I know that Brave Wolf, father of Strong Wolf and grandfather of Smiling Fawn, will be well pleased." With that, she patted the old man's right hand, stood, and walked out into the bright sunlight of spring.

GOING HOME

GOING HOME

B rave Wolf stood at the door to his son's lodge. Over his deerskin shirt and trousers, he wore a short bearskin jacket. He held his favorite pipe in one hand, holding the jacket closed with the other. He had come to speak with his only son about tribal matters.

The day was bright and warm, but the old man's shoulders ached. Too many nights sleeping on a thin mat, *he thought.* Perhaps a few more pine boughs placed on the floor of my lodge would give me some relief.

"Strong Wolf," he called, "it is your father."

A voice replied from within the lodge. "Father, please come into the lodge."

Brave Wolf entered the lodge and saw White Sparrow sitting alone near the fire mending a woven mat.

"Strong Wolf has gone with others," she said. "In search of the rogue bear that has been in the village garden."

White Sparrow was his son's wife and mother of Smiling Fawn. Even in the fifty-fifth year of her life, she was one of the most beautiful of the Armaha women. Brave Wolf

remembered how his son had agonized over her, certain she would reject his show of interest.

White Sparrow and Brave Wolf nodded and clasped hands in greeting in the manner of the Armaha, and the old man sat opposite her on a mat decorated with Brother Sun.

"I am sorry you find my husband is not here. There is some warm broth in the cooking pot. It will make you warm."

She put her mending aside, poured broth into a dark wooden bowl and handed it to Brave Wolf.

"Thank you, my daughter," said the old man. "I will stay only a short while. Perhaps Strong Wolf will be in his lodge later today." He took a sip, and with surprise said, "The soup you have made, it tastes just like my mother's."

"Yes, my father," the woman responded. "It is made the way Sanchea would have made it. But I did not make it. Smiling Fawn is the one."

"I see," said the old man, with a smile on his face. "And where is my granddaughter? If her father is away, perhaps she has some time for me."

Without warning, Smiling Fawn came running into the lodge, went straight to her grandfather, and wrapped her arms around him.

"Smiling Fawn!" said her mother sternly. "You must remember who you are and how you must act. Now let your grandfather enjoy his broth."

"I am sorry, Mother," said the girl as she stepped away from the old man. "But when I heard Grandfather's voice, I, well, I . . ."

White Sparrow looked directly at her daughter and without smiling nodded for her to be silent and to sit. When Smiling Fawn was seated, her mother turned to Brave Wolf. "I too am sorry, Father. My daughter and I will speak of this when we are alone."

"Perhaps my eager granddaughter would like to hear a story about hummingbirds," said Brave Wolf.

"Please excuse me, Father," said White Sparrow as she rose. "I must speak with some of the women in the village. I hope my daughter enjoys your story."

When her mother had stepped outside, Smiling Fawn said, "But I have heard that story, my grandfather."

"You have heard one story about the hummingbird, Nuluk," he said. "But this story is much different. If you will take the bowl from me, I can begin. The broth is very good, my granddaughter."

Smiling Fawn put the bowl aside and sat next to her grandfather. The lines in his face seemed deeper somehow, but his voice was strong and his eyes were clear. She could see him smile as he began to speak.

The flock of hummingbirds flew high and fast. It was spring, and they were returning home from the warmth of lands far away. Sometime before, when the cold air had come to their home and the mountains turned white, they had made their way to these faraway lands. That when Brother Sun rode low in the sky and made sharp, long shadows on the ground. Sister Moon had shown her full face almost five times since the flock had been away. But

when their leader—his name was Sarak—saw that Brother Sun was mounting ever higher for his daily journey, he sensed it was time to fly again, and so they did.

First, they crossed a rugged mountain range, strung out in a long chain near the endless, peaceful sea. The air was warm where they had nested but turned colder as they climbed aloft. Sarak called to them to keep going, encouraging even the youngest to stay with the flock. He had lost many stragglers on their last long flight and worried that the same would happen again. After the mountains, the flock flew above a broad plain reaching as far as the eye could see. Sarak led them down toward trees and grasses where they could look for food. Many in the flock were exhausted from the flight over the mountains. He found the river valley he knew from other journeys and alit in a tree near its banks. The flock followed, and soon the tree was a swirl of activity and noise as the birds flitted about and chattered excitedly. Every bird in the flock had flown safely over the mountains. Now it was time to find nectar, spiders, and small insects to rebuild their strength for the next part of the journey. They would remain in this place until Brother Sun had crossed the sky two times.

The next part of the journey took the flock away from the endless plain, across a wide river and a dense jungle that clung to its banks. Even when the river itself was hidden, the deep green ribbon that was the jungle showed the river's path. Next, they crossed a low mountain range bordered by a sloping plain that led to the warm sea, the one they would have to cross. Once again, Sarak led them to food in a meadow on the shores of a broad lake. It would be their last chance to regain their strength before crossing the sea.

Nuluk had made this journey once before. After leaving the nest where he was born, he had travelled many miles and many days following a broad river that led to a warm sea and then to a valley at the foot of a mountain. It was there Nuluk joined a flock of other hummingbirds. Soon after, the flock made their way to a warmer place, a place far away from the snow and cold of winter. Nuluk had flown with the flock across the broad, warm sea.

With Brother Sun moving higher in the sky, it was time to fly once again. And Nuluk remembered well the long hours in the air, the ache in his wings, the sight of other birds falling from the sky, the feeling of exhaustion, and the thought that he couldn't go on. But he had conquered his fatigue and his fear and had lived to make this journey. As he clung to a tree branch, Nuluk saw that the entire flock was around him. It gave him great comfort to be with so many of his own, this shimmering green flock with dots of red here and there. He often wondered how many were in his flock, but was satisfied knowing only that it was a large number.

He followed Sarak's instructions and flew to the low-lying flowers that covered the meadow before

them. The nectar was warm and sweet. As he bore his long beak into the flowers and drank, Nuluk felt his strength returning. A small spider was spinning a web among the flowers, too busy to see Nuluk, and became a snack for the young bird. He fed on the flowers, insects, and spiders for the whole day and slept peacefully that night. Once, when Sister Moon shone bright in the night sky, Nuluk awoke. He was surprised to see another hummingbird perched close beside him. It was Tama. She and Nuluk had spent much time together on the other side of the mountains. Maybe they would build a nest together when this journey was done. What more could a young hummingbird want? He was with his flock, and a prospective mate perched on the same branch next to him. These were all comforting thoughts, and he slept once again with joy in his heart.

The light of Brother Sun reflected sharply off the water of the lake and awakened Nuluk. He turned his head to see if Tama was awake, but she had gone. He looked around a bit and spied her flitting among the flowers. How gracefully she moved. Nuluk always darted from flower to flower or from place to place, while Tama seemed to flow, to glide as she moved. Nuluk watched her for a moment, let out a sigh, and flew to join her.

"You slept a long time, Nuluk. You must have been very tired," said Tama as he flew to her side. "Perhaps you didn't hear Sarak."

Nuluk was a bit confused "No . . . I . . . Did Sarak speak to us?"

"Yes, silly." Tama spoke softly but made sure Nuluk understood. "He arose before Brother Sun appeared across the lake, and Sarak was quite insistent that we begin feeding. We have a long flight ahead of us and it begins tomorrow. I hope you can find enough nectar."

Nuluk listened closely to what she said, but he was not ready for some female bird—even Tama—to tell him what he should be doing. He rose up on his legs, spread his wings, and lifted his head so she could see the red of his throat. "I will be ready," he said with a touch of anger. "Don't you worry about me,"

"But I do . . ." And Nuluk flew away. ". . . worry about you," Tama said to herself. *He is being stubborn, just like a male hummingbird,* she thought.

"Tama, is she the girl hummingbird from the other story?" asked Smiling Fawn.

"Yes, that is true," said Brave Wolf.

"Will Tama and Nuluk build a nest together?" she asked.

Brave Wolf thought for a moment, and said, "You are full of questions, little one. Perhaps if you wait, your questions will all be answered."

"Grandfather," she said. "You know I do not like the name 'little one.' Why do you use it now?"

"Only this, little . . . my granddaughter," he replied. "The way one acts is the way others respond. Do you understand?"

"Yes, my grandfather," she said quietly with head bowed. Slowly, Smiling Fawn raised her head and looked at Brave Wolf. "Please go on, Grandfather. I know there is much to be learned from these stories."

"You really are who I thought you were," he said. "Good! Now, where was I?"

Smiling Fawn responded slowly, "Nuluk was being stubborn and Tama worried about him."

"Ah, yes," said the old man.

The day started out warm, a gentle breeze moving about in the trees and bushes, causing the lush flowers and grasses to bend and sway this way and that. The flock of hummingbirds moved easily about the meadow as they readied themselves for tomorrow. When Sister Moon next fades away and Brother Sun takes her place in the sky, they would begin the long flight over the warm sea. This would be a test for all of them. Even the strongest would be pushed to their limits. Sarak flew among them, reminding them to eat and to drink, encouraging them, and scolding them when needed. It was his flock to lead and protect. He wanted all to survive the long flight, but knew in his heart some may not. Still he kept on, reminding, encouraging, scolding, and leading.

By the time Brother Sun rode at the highest point of his daily journey, the air had become hot, the

breeze almost nowhere to be felt. The hummingbirds looked for insects and spiders in the shade of large bushes or trees, seeking nectar only from flowers that were near the shade. Some rested high in the trees, trying to enjoy what little breeze they could find.

At last, Brother Sun was lower in the sky and the air cooled down. Once again, the birds were able to move among the flowers in the meadow, sipping their nectar and finding other food. From a distance, it looked like hard work, but to the hummingbirds, it was a joyous time. They knew that soon after the long flight across the warm sea they would be home once more.

Nuluk drank and ate until he thought he would burst. Although it was almost an effort to fold his wings at his side, the extra weight he had gained would provide the energy he needed to cross the warm sea. As Brother Sun gave way to Sister Moon, Nuluk flew among the flowers looking for a few more sips of nectar. Sister Moon appeared smaller this night, a sign that time was moving on. Her silver light reflected off the surface of the lake as if precious stones had been strewn upon it. Nuluk watched the shimmering water until he could no longer hold his eyes open. He slept soundly, perched high above the ground, dreaming of the place he was born, the place he knew as home.

It was a wonderful place, home. There was Rega, his sister, standing on a tree branch urging him to fly

to her, actually teasing him. Rega was older by two days and had been flying for almost a week when Nuluk finally ventured from their nest. His first flight was a short one to be sure, but still it was a flight. Then he learned from his mother and father the ways of the hummingbird. They taught so carefully. He saw Rega fly far away from the nest, turning only once before disappearing among the trees and bushes. He needed to call to her, to ask when she would return. "Rega," he called. "Rega."

"Nuluk!" It was Tama. She repeated his name, nudged him gently with her long, slender beak. "Wake up, Nuluk. You are dreaming."

He awakened with a start, his eyes and mind still hazy from the sound sleep. "I *was* dreaming. And how did you know?"

Tama replied softly, "Many times I have heard you call for this . . . this *Rega* in your sleep." She tried to say it flatly, but her voice betrayed the little female.

"Oh," replied Nuluk, trying to explain. "Rega is my sister . . ." He was still confused. "Did I speak her name? Out *loud*?" He thought for a moment and went on. "It was a dream, a dream of when I first learned to fly . . . and Rega flew away. I have not seen her since."

Tama was relieved. With a lilt in her voice she said, "Perhaps you will see her after we cross the warm sea . . . when we are home. Quickly, one last time among the flowers because Sarak says we will

fly when Brother Sun shines fully on the lake. And that will be soon."

In the early morning light, the two young hummingbirds descended from their perch and once again flitted among the flowers at the edge of the lake. As the sky changed colors from deep blue to saffron and pink, the flock buzzed noisily, knowing that Brother Sun would soon begin his daily journey. At once, the edge of the orange ball peeked over a distant hill and spread the surface of the lake with golden light.

Sarak swooped among them and said one word: "Now!"

The flock of hummingbirds rose in the air and turned toward the warm sea they knew was but a short distance away. Soon they were flying above its surface, no stopping until they reached the distant shore. The air was cool and fresh, and the hummingbirds were strong and ready for the flight. They called to one another as they flew faster and faster. The flock was strung out for almost a mile, each bird but a faint blur as they sped toward home, keeping close to the gentle waves rolling over the warm sea.

As Brother Sun rose higher and higher in the sky, and the air became warmer, they could see a wall of gray mist hanging before them over the warm sea. Instead of blue, the sky had a strange green cast to it. Sarak had heard about the gray mist and green sky, and the danger they held. He called to the birds near him to follow as he flew away from the wall of gray. Upward and upward he led them—farther away from the gathering storm. The warm air above the sea became cool then cold. There had been only a gentle breeze when they first took flight. Now the wind gusted at them, seeming to push them toward the wall of mist. As they rose higher, they could see clearly below them the white crested waves being driven by the wind.

In the next instant, the air was filled with rain that soaked the flock. The hummingbirds found they had to work harder to stay in the air. Sensing the great danger, Sarak flew downward toward the surface, hoping to find a place for the flock to land, a chance to find shelter from the wind and rain. He spied what looked to be a small island and pointed his long bill in that direction. The trusting flock followed. Next came hail, hard crystal pellets that tore through the flock, knocking many out of the sky. They were almost to the island when the wind swirled among them flinging them in every direction: a few toward the island, some far out over the sea, others into the stormy waters below.

Nuluk found himself high in the air, alone. He hovered for a moment to clear his head and to find the direction he should go. Another bird sped by him, but it wasn't flying; it was being carried by the wind toward the heart of the storm. Then the other bird took control, trying its best to resist the pull of the storm. Nuluk noticed how gracefully the other hummingbird flew.

Tama! he thought. He yelled to her, "Dive, Tama! Follow me!"

In the next instant she was gone. Nuluk dove toward the surface of the sea, hoping to see the rest of the flock. Once or twice he interrupted his dive to

hover, looking to see if Tama was following. But when he finally spied the island and the other birds, he realized he was alone. No one was following.

"*Grandfather,*" *said Smiling Fawn.* "*Why are your stories always so sad? Tama was hoping that she and Nuluk could make a home together. But she is lost.*"

"*Remember what I have told you,*" *he said.* "*Life can be joyous, and it can be cruel. So it is with legends and stories such as this, for they are reflections of the real world.*"

"*But to be lost in such a terrible storm,*" *she said.* "*I know I shouldn't be sad, but I am.*"

"*You have a tender heart, my granddaughter,*" *he said softly.* "*And that is good, indeed. Shall I go on?*"

"*Yes, Grandfather,*" *she said.* "*Please go on.*"

Brave Wolf put an arm around Smiling Fawn and drew her close. His granddaughter was in the fifteenth year of her life. Moments like this would not happen often.

Nuluk found Sarak perched in a low bush close to the ground, protected from the rain and hail. Sarak's eyes were closed, and his head, once held proudly high, hung limply from his neck. He told Nuluk that the flock numbered only a few. They had trusted him, and he had failed.

Very softly, Nuluk said, "It was the storm."

Sarak looked up through saddened eyes and replied, "But I am the leader . . . I am responsible . . ." He could not finish.

"Try to get some rest," replied Nuluk. "Perhaps tomorrow we can continue the long flight home." He moved to another branch, leaving Sarak with his grief.

With Sarak in the lead, the small flock of hummingbirds rose in the air and flew away from the small island. They had been there three days, huddled in low bushes while the storm raged above and around them. The fourth day dawned bright and clear, with a gentle breeze to stir the few trees and bushes on the island. Almost aimlessly, Sarak led them across a narrow stretch of the warm sea toward the dun-colored land on its shores. The storm had sapped his energy and destroyed his confidence. To Nuluk, it felt as if they had no leader at all. He flew to the front of the flock and joined Sarak.

Nuluk spoke. "Which way is home?"

The older hummingbird responded, "I do not know. I do not know. We are close to the warm sea, but the land below is wrong, all wrong."

"The storm has brought us here," said Nuluk. "You know the way home. You must know the way home."

Almost crying, Sarak answered, "I do not know. I do not know." Without a word, Sarak let his head drop and fell to the ground. Not a word, not a gesture. He simply fell. The flock flew to their fallen leader and stood on the ground looking at the motionless body. One hopped over to Sarak and nudged him with her bill, but Sarak had left the world to be with the Great One.

The flock became a buzz of twittering, asking each other what will happen now, how they will find home, and finally, who would lead them. At length they all turned to Nuluk and waited. After a moment Mesak, another young male spoke. "You, Nuluk, you lead us home."

"But I do not . . ." Nuluk began.

Mesak interrupted. "We want you to lead us. We give you our trust." The rest of the flock echoed the words, trying to encourage Nuluk.

Reluctantly, he responded: "I will do my best. That is all I can promise. Now, let us move Sarak to a place that gives respect to his life.

Mesak and two other hummingbirds flew to the lifeless body and pushed it with their bills until it lay in the shade of a low-growing cactus that was covered with bright yellow flowers.

Nuluk watched, and when they were finished, he said, "Good. All right, follow close. Let us go home."

The flock rose in the air together and hovered as Nuluk found the direction he thought would lead them home. He motioned to them, and they began

once again to fly through the air, one following another as they had before. When Brother Sun stood directly overhead, the land curved away from them, and they flew across the warm sea once more. As Sister Moon began to take her brother's place in the sky, the flock settled by a broad, slow-moving river. Nuluk was relieved that everyone in his little band had made the flight safely. He thought to himself, *Perhaps I can lead them home. All I need to do now is find it!* He had other thoughts but lost them as darkness fell and sleep took over.

After crossing the river, the flock flew toward the place where Brother Sun appears each day. There they found a broad, green valley that looked familiar. They were excited to be home, and spent much time flitting from tree to tree and flying to the ends of the valley. Nuluk was unsure. The place looked like home, but it didn't *feel* like home. But the flock was so content, he said nothing, choosing instead to watch and to wait. It didn't take long.

Three days after arriving at the valley, Nuluk was sitting on the branch of a live oak tree among the fronds of moss that hung from it. He heard a rush of noise and looked to see a large bird of some sort settling on a branch above him. Its feathers were dark brown in color with hints of gold. Its eyes were brown and large, and rimmed with yellow; they seemed to look through Nuluk. The bird's beak was curved and pointed. And the yellow talons at the end of its thin legs looked to be strong and sharp. Nuluk realized the bird was an eagle.

"Are you new in this valley?" the eagle said. The words were drawn out like long loops in the air. Nuluk didn't respond so the large bird repeated, speaking louder, "Are you new here?"

"Yes," Nuluk finally replied. Then added, "Yes, I am."

"I didn't mean only you," said the eagle. "I mean all of you. All of you tiny, little birds." The large bird spread his wings out angrily as he spoke.

"Oh," said Nuluk. "You mean the whole flock."

"Of course I mean the whole flock!" The eagle hopped onto the branch next to Nuluk.

Nuluk tried to stay calm, to hide his fear. "I am sorry if I upset you. You surprised me. Yes, my flock and I are new here. We flew into the valley this morning." Hesitantly he added, "This is our home."

"Enough!" The eagle laughed. "Listen to what you say. You say you are home. Listen carefully. I am Varn the eagle, and this is *my* valley. Any birds or animals in this valley do as I tell them. I tell them where they can live, and I tell them where they can hunt. Do you understand?"

"Yes, I understand, but . . ." Nuluk began.

The eagle interrupted. "Listen to what I have said and heed what I tell you. That is the way it will be in *my* valley." With that, the eagle flew away, directly over Nuluk's head. Nuluk could see clearly the sharp talons as the large bird "whooshed" above him.

"Varn? But, Grandfather," said Smiling Fawn, "where is Shinaka? She rules the skies and protects the green valley, our green valley."

"That is true," he said.

"Then where is Shinaka?" asked the young woman.

Brave Wolf smiled and chuckled. "Just listen, my granddaughter. The story still has a ways to go."

A few days later, Mesak found Nuluk feeding among a bed of fading flowers. "Nuluk, there you are. Something has happened. You should come see."

Without hesitation, Nuluk followed Mesak to a pond where the small flock was gathered around the lifeless body of one of their own. The little bird looked oddly peaceful, but its eyes stared at nothing.

Nuluk waited and Mesak spoke. "She drank water from the pond and flew among the flowers here. She said something about a funny taste, and then her life ended. We think something is wrong with the water."

Nuluk told them, "We have found other water that we can drink. Let us stay away from this pond. Stay close together for a few days. There are things I need to do." Then, nodding toward the dead bird. "And find a suitable place for our little friend." Nuluk saw they understood, so he rose in the air to learn more about this strange valley.

Brother Sun crossed the sky five times while he was gone from the flock. And when he returned to

them, Nuluk had learned all he needed to know about the place they were calling home. He told about birds and animals he met that only existed instead of truly living; and about pools of water that looked clear and pure, but had an odd taste; about flowers that seemed to have lost their color. And he told them about Varn the eagle who ruled the valley as his own. When he had finished, the flock fell silent, looking at one another with fear-filled eyes.

Mesak spoke first. "We cannot stay here, Nuluk. We hoped this would be our home, but it is not."

Nuluk said to them, "I will find a home for us."

That set the flock to twittering excitedly about finding their real home, how sweet the flowers and their nectar would be, how peaceful their lives would be. All the while Nuluk remained silent, unsure if he could keep his promise.

Early the next day, Nuluk told the flock to stay close to Mesak, to follow his instructions, and to stay away from the other animals and birds in the valley, especially Varn. All was agreed, and Nuluk rose in the air to a spot just above a tree with limp, graying leaves. There he hovered while deciding which direction to go. Then, with Brother Sun shining on his right shoulder, Nuluk began to fly.

After Brother Sun and Sister Moon had made three journeys across the sky, Nuluk found himself looking down at a broad valley covered with stately trees, fields of dark green grass, and lakes too many to count, all glistening with the reflected light from

Brother Sun. He spied a large patch of bright orange flowers and wondered how their nectar might taste. He imagined it would be warm and sweet. So he glided down to the patch and began sampling. And it was as he had thought. The songs of birds and the sounds of animals filled the air. The air, yes, the air. It carried the sweet odors of earth and spice. It was truly a delightful place to be, this green valley. As he flitted from one flower to another, Nuluk thought, *This could be our home. Yes, I think it could be.*

As Nuluk made his way among the bright orange flowers, sipping nectar and enjoying the warmth of Brother Sun, a large hawk with an orange head soared high above him, watching.

"Now we are back at the beginning," said Smiling Fawn excitedly. *"When Nuluk met Shinaka. What a wondrous story, Grandfather."*

"And what have you learned from the story, little . . . my granddaughter?" he asked.

"I am not sure, but I will try," she said as she tilted her head to one side. After a moment, Smiling Fawn went on. *"A true leader accepts whatever the Great One offers and does the best he can."*

"Or she can," he said.

"Yes," she said, smiling. *"Whatever she can. Whatever I can. For I cannot change the reality of the world around me."*

"You have learned well, my granddaughter," said the old man. *"If you will help me to my feet, I will leave you*

with your thoughts, and I will walk down by the river to watch the water roll between the banks and among the rocks, for that is not so different from our lives."

Smiling Fawn stood at the door to her father's lodge and watched as Brave Wolf, holding tight to his walking stick, made his way slowly through the village, stopping now and then to have a kind word for each man, woman, and child he met along the way.

THE PLEDGE

THE PLEDGE

High above the trees, the great hawk flew in wide circles, watching the rider and pony as they made their way along the riverbank, casting long shadows across the swiftly flowing stream. It was late in the day, and Brother Sun would soon have found his way across the great arc of the sky, once again allowing the stars and Sister Moon to take his place.

The pony is young, sturdy; his coat is shiny and deep red, like the leaves of a scarlet oak in summer, a streak of white slashing across his right eye and down to his muzzle. He runs easily along the grassy bank and tosses his head from side to side. It is a sign of pure joy. The pony has no name, for the rider has not yet given him one; he was a present from her father on her last birthday, the sixteenth of her life. The rider is Smiling Fawn, daughter of Strong Wolf and White Sparrow, an obedient young woman of the Armaha tribe with a sense of joy and independence that often confounds her parents. As she rides, her long, black hair streams behind her like a banner declaring freedom, echoing the dark mane of her pony, for she rides for the pure pleasure of it and for the bond she feels with her new friend, the pony. At these moments, Smiling Fawn feels an unspeakable sense

of freedom. Freedom from care, from responsibility. Freedom to think about her life and to dream.

She wears a doeskin shirt and trousers made for her by her mother. The soft leather, once tan, is now almost white, bleached by long days in the sun. The trousers are decorated with fringe along the outer seams and a row of bright beads at the cuff of each leg. Those same beads of red, blue, yellow, and orange are sewn onto the front and back of the shirt. A single piece of pure gold on a leather thong hangs around her neck and flies this way and that as Smiling Fawn rides. And as she rides, she leans forward so the pony will hear words she learned from her grandfather, Brave Wolf:

> *Our people feel a kinship with the world;*
>
> *The place the Great One gave us to defend.*
>
> *We honor all the ancients from our past*
>
> *And promise to remember how to live.*

Hearing the young woman, the great hawk, Shinaka, silently glides closer to enjoy the pure, sweet voice and the words. Shinaka has heard the words many times, first from Sanchea, then her son, Brave Wolf. It is more a prayer, words of great beauty and importance, and often recited by the Armaha, the people who help her guard and protect the Green Valley.

Now Smiling Fawn continues:

> *High mountain, great Umaqua, hear my voice*
>
> *And take this pledge I offer now to you:*

To live a life of truth and careful thought

That pleases you, our only Sacred House.

It was almost an hour later when Brave Wolf watched anxiously as his granddaughter walked slowly into the village, a smile on her perfect face, leading her new pony while feeding it pieces of an apple. That was just like Smiling Fawn, always showing gratitude. But the hour was late; a soft glow illuminated the evening sky that Brother Sun had left some time ago. And that was the source of his anxiety: A young woman—especially his own granddaughter—should not be away from the village when darkness comes. Smiling Fawn offered the last piece of apple to the pony and looked up, surprised to see her grandfather in front of his lodge. His look was stern, unsmiling, direct. She lowered her eyes and frowned, at once understanding his anger.

"You have been riding again," said Brave Wolf. He waited, expressionless, for her response.

"Y . . . yes, my grandfather," Smiling Fawn replied softly. She felt awkward, unsure, shifting her weight from one foot to the other.

"I am here, little one," he said, knowing how she disliked that name. "I am not on the ground where you want to look."

She raised her head and looked into his eyes. "I . . . I am sorry," she whispered.

Brave Wolf told himself to be strict, to make her understand her error. But this was Smiling Fawn, the child he had treasured from the day of her birth, the little girl he had guided for so long, the young woman for whom he had such

great hopes. He appraised Smiling Fawn silently. Finally, gathering the strength he needed, he spoke in a voice that she had heard only a few times, a voice that told her to obey without question. He said, "Take your pony to his hitching post, tell your mother and your father that you are in the village, and then come to my lodge. And bring an extra blanket; it will be cool when the stars light the sky."

She did as she was told and returned to Brave Wolf's lodge. She stood just outside the entrance, now covered with a large bearskin.

In a small voice she asked, "Grandfather, may I come into your lodge?"

"Yes," he replied. And Smiling Fawn entered the lodge.

An unsmiling Brave Wolf was sitting cross-legged on a small woven mat facing the door, a blanket of red and orange around his shoulders. The smoke from his favorite pipe floated gently about his face and head. He gestured to a mat to his right, this one decorated with the likeness of the great hawk, and Smiling Fawn lowered herself to it, tucked her legs under herself and placed the blanket she carried next to her. She looked directly at the old man, folded her hands in her lap and waited. They sat without speaking for some minutes.

When she could hold back no longer, Smiling Fawn pleaded, "My grandfather, I want to say . . ."

"No!" he said sharply, interrupting her. "It is I who will speak." Then, with a gentler voice, he said, "I want to tell you a story, my granddaughter. It will take only a little time. Shall I begin?"

Smiling Fawn nodded silently. And the old man began to speak in soft, even tones.

Long ago, it is told, there was a small tribe called the Chare. They lived in a valley much like the green valley we call home, but I cannot tell you where it was. Theirs was a good life, a contented life. They had learned to plant vegetables, as we do, and to raise cattle and horses. They had even tamed a few wild pigs and bred them for meat. The streams and lakes nearby provided a great number of fish, and the forest was full of deer and other game. Yes, it was a good and contented life for the Chare.

The Chare were a pleasant, light-hearted people. They always enjoyed singing and dancing, storytelling, and festivals. In one year, it is told, the Chare honored days on end with a celebration of one kind or another. Of course, while they were celebrating, the many tasks needed for daily living were forgotten. Women were too busy to wash clothing or to bring water to the village. Children had no time for simple chores like folding sleeping mats or feeding the horses or pulling weeds from among the vegetables in the village garden. The men spent so much time telling stories to each other that no one thought to hunt for game in the forest or to bring fish home from the lake or nearby streams.

As the story is told, the celebrations went on until someone realized the cow wasn't giving milk or there was no bread or the horses looked starved. Then the Chare would scurry around tending to all the tasks that had been ignored for the longest time.

Smiling Fawn looked at Brave Wolf with surprise on her face, and said, "Grandfather?"

"Yes, my child?" he said. His eyes twinkled with the trace of a smile at the corners of his mouth.

"You call them the Chare," she said. "I do not remember that word. What is it?"

"It is simply the name of the tribe," he said. "May I go on?"

"Yes, my grandfather," she said.

"Put that blanket around you," he said, bringing an end to her questions.

As she wrapped the blanket around herself, he continued . . .

After tending to all the many forgotten responsibilities, you can imagine that the Chare were tired, very tired indeed. And so they would rest for a few days. While they were resting, they would be thinking about all the singing and dancing and storytelling, all the things they had enjoyed for so long. Sooner or later, one or two would start to sing, or someone would begin to tell a story. Before too long it was all enjoyment, and the work to be done was forgotten once again. It was a cycle that repeated itself like the turning of the seasons.

The Great One took notice of all this, and was saddened by it. *What can I do?* thought the Great One. *I want them to be free, to find what is right and what is wrong, to make a good life for their people.* But that was not enough. No. The Chare needed to see what they were doing, how they were destroying their own tribe. They needed to be shown.

The oldest member of the tribe was a man called Dyami, for he was named for Brother Eagle. He always wore a single eagle feather in his hair. Another eagle feather decorated his favorite pipe, which he carried with him every day. It seemed that his face was eternally shrouded in smoke. He was a wise and serious man, having lived many years among his people. There had been a time when the Chare went to Dyami for counsel and advice, when he taught the young girls and boys of the tribe what it meant to be a Chare. But now, he was just an old man, unnoticed, unregarded by the tribe, a relic from the past. And the Great One chose Dyami to be his messenger.

On a warm, still night, the Great One spoke to Dyami as he sat by the front of his lodge. It was his habit to smoke one last pipe each night before retiring to his sleeping mat. He would sit on the stump of a tree he had felled many years before when only a boy—something his father said he could not do—and watch the stars begin to take their place high above.

"Dyami, my son," said a strange, quiet voice.

"Yes," he said, expecting to see someone approaching.

"No one is coming, Dyami," said the voice. "It is I, the Great One. There is little time, so listen to what I say."

Dyami had heard stories about the Great One speaking to humans, so he listened. "Tell me what you want to say," he said.

"I feel great sorrow for you and your people," said the voice. "They forget to care for Mother Earth. They care only to frolic and enjoy life without honoring it. Tell them this: If they act like children, I will treat them like children. Tell them that."

"I will," said Dyami. He waited for a response; there was none.

"I am sorry, Grandfather, I must speak!" Smiling Fawn said excitedly."

"I didn't know my story would come to this," said Brave Wolf. And he laughed heartily.

"Oh, Grandfather," she said. "It's just that I want to know the name . . . Chare . . . the word. Is it from Kiowa, or Dakota?"

"Or from Techlit, perhaps?" he asked. He had spoken with a lilt in his voice and an unapologetic smile on his face. He put his right hand out, and Smiling Fawn eagerly took it in hers.

"Yes, Techlit!" she said. "The tribe and language of your mother, my great grandmother, Sanchea." Smiling Fawn beamed as she spoke. "The name, the word Chare, means young one, or innocent one."

"What else might it mean?" asked Brave Wolf.

180

"It might mean child," said Smiling Fawn.

"So you remember," he said, pleased that his grand-daughter had not forgotten. "Now, what does the story mean? What does it mean for you?"

Smiling Fawn tilted her head to one side and thought for a moment. It was a habit she carried from her earliest years.

He thought, She is a young woman, but still my "little one."

Finally, she responded, "If I act like a child, you will treat me like a child . . . like the Great One and the Chare."

"And . . ." he said, leading her further.

Without hesitation, Smiling Fawn answered with confidence. "And if I act like a responsible young woman, you will treat me with earned respect."

They sat together quietly for a few minutes. Then Brave Wolf said, "Help me up, my granddaughter, and let me take you to the lodge of your parents. It is not every day that I get to walk with such a respected member of our tribe."

As Sister Moon began her journey across the sky, Brave Wolf rose, took the arm his granddaughter offered, and walked slowly but proudly with her through the village.

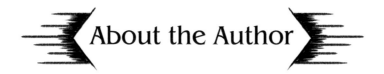

About the Author

C harles B. Pettis writes short stories and poems, mostly for his own enjoyment. He is the author of the self-published book *Scraps of Paper*, which was produced primarily for family and friends. *The Hummingbird and the Hawk* is his first venture into commercial publication. Mr. Pettis and his wife live in Roswell, Georgia.

You can contact him at cbpvoice@aol.com.